Summary

In the 21st century most people have a skewered view of politics and politicians. What we see of them and the antics they pull often shames their authoritative position within our societies. But what's it really like from the inside where the action is. Do any of those individuals really have an easy time of things or does a dog-eat-dog scenario that we've often seen portrayed create an environment that for many would prove unbearable.

TABLE OF CONTENTS

Chapter 1 *Awkward Youth*

Chapter 2 (P. 34) *Cabinet Meeting – for the good of the country*

Chapter 3 (P.74) *The cost of an extra-marital relationship*

Chapter 4 (P.116) *The power of public funding*

Chapter 5 (P.153) *The possibility of a problem*

Chapter 6 (P.182) *Unexpected allies*

Chapter 7 (P.248) *Unknown Depths*

Acknowledgement

To Peter Burles who acted as an ideas man and kept us moving along at a good pace.

CHAPTER ONE

Awkward youth

The Evening News headline stunned Prime Minister Rupert Streaker. The reports of decades-old events, when he, as a young university student, had participated in outrageous behaviour with his friends, as a means of self-expression, seemed nothing extraordinary. So, political rivalry seemed to be the only plausible reason the newspaper appeared to be making their antics sound so deplorable. Irritated rather than annoyed, Streaker, sat behind a large mahogany desk in his office at Number 10, continued reading the article until a personal secret he hoped would remain lost in the past unexpectedly appeared. A cold chill ran down his spine. Sex! One of three snares that could pull the rug from underneath any politician, the others being dipping into the public purse and going to war without justification. The latter two had been normalised to some extent by his string of predecessors and senior ministers, who paid the ultimate price by standing down for re-election – at least for the next six months, by which time the public memory would have moved on.

Sex, however, was much more personal and hence easier to manipulate to appear far worse than what had occurred. Especially if there were witnesses. Unfortunately, in this instance his entire class had been present, photographs possibly taken. A good day had suddenly turned sour.

Streaker was well-known for his charisma at winning over the ladies. Even as he slipped into his mid-forties, he had retained much of his beguiling boyish appeal, and his alluring combination of dark hair, blue eyes, and fair skin worked their magic any time he willed it to. He often wished he was taller though. At five feet six he could easily find himself lost in a crowd. Not a good thing when meeting with his European counterparts who enjoyed looking down at him as they stood side by side. Social distancing due to COVID had done much to alleviate this concern. *At least it proved good for something*, he often caught himself thinking. Snatching up the phone, he dialled his number one fixer: Jonathon Bandip. 'Get in here now. It's an emergency.'

Bandip was there within the minute. Tall, handsome, and immaculately dressed, he looked every bit a top-level super-smooth media liaison consultant per his job remit. Of course, he had also been in the same class as the prime minister, at a private college of note and, therefore, possessed the same articulation and mindset. Cynics suggested that their schooling was bent on clone creation. Not that anyone who mattered took any notice, as they too would have been a product of the same schooling.

'Kate Allfores!' Streaker grumbled. 'Of all the people to suddenly show up as an old sex conquest! The evening paper has us splashed all over it.'

'I'd forgotten about that little tryst you had with her. Gosh that was a long time ago. How on earth did it suddenly crop up?'

'Well, it bloody has!' Streaker sat back in his large leather chair – the throne of power in the UK.

'She's on the front bench', Bandip added, as if Streaker could have forgotten that piece of information. Lifting the newspaper from the desk, his eyes widened at the photograph with blurred naked bodies and unblurred faces. Allfores gripping a cross in her hands, kneeling on a table, her lover pressed against her rear.

'I know where she is, damnit!' Streaker shifted uncomfortably in his chair.

'Had we been in France, you'd be considered a hero of some sort.' Bandip moved the paper around to catch extra light from the window.

'We're not in France, Jonathon! This is the bloody UK where cavorting while being married is considered a heinous crime!'

'But you weren't married then. Besides, I can easily claim that it's a Photoshop mock-up. Fake news.'

'You could, but few people other than her husband know she has a tattoo of Lassie on her left buttock.'

His track record as a womaniser at university had won him the well-deserved nickname 'Magic-Streak'. The male student with the most notches on his gun. It was a proud boast that would be deemed extremely politically incorrect today.

Bandip studied the photograph. 'Ah yes. Oh, well, that's a good thing. She's a dog lover and the UK is full of them.'

'My wife likes dogs, but she's won't bloody appreciate my shagging Allfores just because she's a dog lover!'

'I take it you've never told her about Allfores?'

'What do you think?'

'You told me the two of you had an open and honest relationship.'

'We do, but I never got round to mentioning Allfores. To be honest, I didn't see the point. Jessica can be a mite jealous at times and discovering that I'd shagged one of my Under Secretaries of State wouldn't do her any good. She'd be livid I didn't tell her.'

'What about the press?'

'Damn the press! I need you to fix this with Jessica. Can you claim that my face was Photoshopped in?'

'It'll cost you.' Bandip was already calculating the approximate amount of bribe it would take. 'I can't see your scar in this.'

Streaker snatched the paper from him. 'You're right. I had the accident just after.'

'Stuff Photoshop. We can claim it's not you because there's no scar on your arm or shoulder. There's no date stamp on the photo, so there's reasonable doubt. The public will take your side. I'm sure of it. They hate the press making phony claims nearly as much as they hate bankers.'

'Nice one, Jonathon. Just as long as it persuades Jessica that all this is utter nonsense.' He sighed in relief. The fire was almost out before it had properly begun.

'Could cost a bit to check that there are no other images lying in wait to do the dirty.'

'Sod the cost. Once it's done, find out the name of the weasel who took that picture. It has to be someone from the class.'

'I can think of a couple of suspects. Damien Cross or maybe Ian Broome. Neither of them liked you.'

'Do you keep in contact?'

'Of course. They're both doing well. Neither of them ever mentions you though, which is what I find odd, considering you are the prime minister. You'd think they'd ask me something about you, but not a word.'

'And we'll need to move Allfores. Somewhere no one will be able to find her. A job in the basement of some department so she rarely sees the light of day.'

'Yes, of course. I'm sure we can find a suitable position.' Bandip was studying the photograph again. 'She still looks good. Has kept herself very presentable. What is it she's holding?'

'Don't you remember?'

'I was the one keeping watch outside the church', he grumbled. 'Missed it all.'

'It's a crucifix. Turned her on, being shagged on the altar with it. Not that I ever saw an Evangelical church as consecrated ground. All that happy-clappy stuff degrades the solemnity of churches.'

'The Americans love them, mind you.'

'Agreed, but look who's made the most of that. He's been milking it for the past four years and is still getting away with it. You have to give him that.'

'I'm not sure he'll survive much longer. They're beginning to wise up since the COVID thing started. I mean, with more than a hundred and ninety thousand dead, they were bound to start paying attention. Especially because of the lock-down. All they needed do was turn on the TV and watch what politicians were saying and doing. It's the same here. You can't move about without the spotlight being thrown on you. We can't afford another lock-down. Not for the economy but because of all the accompanying public scrutiny.'

'Absolutely agree, Jonathon. This blasted virus has done us more damage than any newspaper ever did. I blame the Chinese.'

'As do the Americans.'

'Thing is, how will the public think of me after a vaccine comes out? They need to like me, Jonathon. History has to show that.' Streaker was fixated on the public's high regard of him, especially when it came to history books being written. He wanted his life to mirror those of his own political heroes such as Churchill and Thatcher – people who left their mark and made, in his eyes at least, the Great British islands a significant dot on the world map. Public adoration was also key to his staying in power. He had witnessed it first-hand with Blair. For two whole terms in office, almost three, Blair had enjoyed public support. Until war with Iraq. Streaker wanted his three full terms in office and often imagined himself listed on Wikipedia beside Stanley Baldwin and Edward Stanley. Like them, the public needed to need him. It was simply a matter of convincing them that they did. Which was where Bandip entered.

'I'm sure it will Rupert, but you must expect a few hiccups. Public opinion is fluid at best. We must stick to our policies at all costs to achieve the agenda Maggie wanted. COVID is temporary, our agenda permanent. That's what we must remember. If you want to continue being liked by the public and supported by the party, then stay on the course. We can't afford to have you losing your nerve at this point just because you want the public to like you. Being popular all the time is impossible for any prime minister. There are always far too many tough decisions that have dire consequences. The best you can hope for is to catch them off guard with some terrific handouts prior to an election so you can snatch a second and even a third time in office if that's your aim.'

'It makes it easier for me to do what's required if they're on my side. I don't want to be hated like the ones who came before me.'

'But you always knew there was a risk it could happen.'

'What about my base supporters? What's their mood at the moment?'

'They're still staunchly behind you. We'll turn this scandal round, and they'll adore you even more. You'll be seen as the underdog, and you know the British public loves nothing better than an underdog.'

Streaker appeared satisfied. Maintaining his boyish charm and sense of fun had always been part of his strategy to win over voters. He needed to be liked, needed it as much as he had to breathe. It made him inexplicably comfortable. As had the feigning to be a bit of a bumbler, which seemingly add to his charm, as supporters laughed and joked with him rather than at him.

'Have you spoken to Allfores about this?'

'No, I haven't dared.'

'My understanding is that she's done pretty well in her job. There were a few surprises considering she was a last-minute choice. It's still a shame she has to go though. We've far too many less capable ones botching things up.'

'How do you think she got the job in the first place?' Streaker grinned. 'Of course, that was before anyone had dug this up. She's still a real wildcat.'

'You didn't! Why, you're an old dog!' Bandip smiled at Streaker with admiration.

'Hence why Jessica must never find out. I'd end up a pauper.' He imagined his jealousy-riddled wife storming through their home. Unthinkable. Frightening. The consequence would be horrendous financially. Streaker pushed aside the thoughts – as though considering them any longer would be reckless– and focused on Bandip.

'I'm sure you're exaggerating, Rupert. She clearly loves you, and then there are the children of course.'

'She'd want to hurt me, Jonathon. A woman scorned and all that… Going for my money and properties would inflict exactly the type of pain she'd want me to experience. Indescribable torture.'

'Gosh, you do surprise me.'

'No time to waste now. Get Allfores gone and start the counterchallenge using Photoshop and my scar as excuses. Let me know how much it's going to cost. See if we can't pay some off with expenses.'

As Bandip stepped out, Bernice Walters, personal assistant to the prime minister, stepped in. A stocky, fifty-something civil servant with a lifetime of experience, she was exactly what she appeared to be: prissy and tough. 'I was out when the evening papers arrived, Rupert. I only just saw the headlines.'

'Already taken care of, Bernice. Complete lie. They Photoshopped me in. I'm totally innocent. Fortunately, they omitted the scars I have on my arm and shoulder from an accident I had when at university. Their mistake. Lucky for me though.'

'Of course, Rupert. These scandalmongers deserve imprisonment. Would you like me to warn Jessica?'

The door behind her suddenly swung open, and Jessica Streaker stormed in – a beauty gripped by anger. Her eyes on fire, long dark hair flowing around her shoulders. Her tight white blouse heaving rapidly. 'Is it true?'

'Jessica, we were just talking about you', Bernice began, slightly intimidated.

'Shut up Bernice! Well?'

Streaker relaxed. A small smile played at the corners of his mouth. 'You sound like you've already made up your mind.'

'Don't play me like the gullible public, Rupert. Did you bang Allfores?'

'Take a closer look at the photo and tell me if I did or didn't.' He turned around the newspaper on his desk for her.

Snatching it up, Jessica studied it closely. 'Your scars.'

'I rest my case', he answered, smug. The relief at missing another silver-bullet was exhilarating.

'Bastards!'

'Indeed, my darling. Such an obvious mistake shows this to be an amateur's work. Don't worry, I'll find out who did this. Then there'll be all hell to pay.'

She rushed round to him took his head in her hands smothering him with kisses before pushing it between her breasts. When her apology was finished, she said, 'Allfores is one of your Under-Secretaries.' .

'She's moving. I can't afford the public suspecting I have any connection with the woman.'

Her smile pleased him. Back on safe ground.

'If I ever find out that you lied to me, I'll cut your balls off.' Jessica said it through her smile.

'I love you, and I love our children. The idea that I had a fling with Allfores is completely absurd.'

'You'd have told me, wouldn't you?' she asked, studying his eyes now. He could almost feel her penetrating gaze touch his soul.

'Why wouldn't I?'

'Maybe because you work with her.' Her seemingly innocuous suggestion full of traps.

'You said it. I work with her. Nothing more.' His tone confident, re-assuring.

She kissed him and left without a word to Walters, the door closing behind her.

'Is there anything you want me to do, Rupert?' Walters asked.

'You know how much I value your opinion, Bernice.' She smiled modestly in response. 'What's your opinion on the nation's current attitude towards the government and, more specifically, me?'

Walters had never been one to hold back when asked a direct question. She was 'old school'. From the stiff upper lip brigade before the lefty loonies had stepped in with their empathy for anyone and everything.

'The public thinks that every politician is looking out for themselves, filling their pockets with public money while the workforce struggles to keep a roof over its head.'

You can't change the habits of a lifetime, Streaker thought. 'How would Maggie have overcome these bad feelings?'

'She'd have started a war.' Her glib reply sounded harsh even to her ears. 'I mean, not directly, but she would have manipulated things for a situation to occur and leave us with no choice. Wars tend to unite a country, common enemy and all that, especially if the foes are deemed barbaric.'

'A war', Streaker thoughtfully said to himself.

'Only trouble is, we've suffered several wars in Afghanistan, Iraq, and the list goes on. Our losses run in the hundreds, and people really want peace. COVID should have served as a common purpose to unite the entire country, but it hasn't happened so far.'

'Why is that?'

'Too many failures on the government's part that can't be blamed on a different party. Well, not easily at least.'

He didn't like Bernice. She was merely a necessary evil. He kept her close because he knew her values wouldn't allow her to betray him. A middle-aged, starched spinster married to the job, with a couple of cats at home, honesty, integrity, and loyalty were her strong suits. She was perfect for the role she played. However, Bandip had warned him to never underestimate her, especially when concocting a plan that veered outside the comfortable zone of his prime ministerial remit. Even Jessica had suggested he get rid of her. That she was too dangerous. But he believed in keeping his enemies closer than he did his friends and used her as a sounding board. Her reactions to his ideas helped him gauge the degree of opposition to expect from political rivals.

Politics was, after all, a game. Highly sophisticated at times but still just a game in all honesty. Streaker had always been good at games, particularly Chess, and was certain of his future moves well ahead of taking the first steps. Planning was paramount to everything he had achieved thus far. Keeping Bernice close was just another part of his grand strategy. Though their relationship was never easy, it was one he valued. His reputation as someone who played fast and loose made her uncomfortable and put her ill at ease. His request that she remain as his personal assistant surprised, possibly even shocked, her. She had accepted the position with a degree of trepidation, after he claimed to need someone honest and with above-average integrity. Her acceptance appeared humble, as if she was completely lost for words. Doing the unexpected had achieved Streaker's goal. Throwing her a curveball, leaving her without any idea of where it was headed, filling her up with reasonable doubt had accomplished his verbal need for her to overwhelm all opposition. People like to be needed; that's how they get comfortable. Staying on in a familiar role and workplace, among familiar people, only under a new boss, was sufficiently straightforward for her to resist any initial urge to move. She may have even believed that things would return to what they had once been. However, Streaker knew something Walter refused to accept: the world had moved on. The political cut and thrust of previous leaders had been replaced by spin, arguably making it a more difficult environment to operate in. Blatantly doing unacceptable things came with its risks. Lying would always be challenged by hard fact. The clever strategy was to fool the public into believing that right was wrong. That black was white. Most of the time, the public wasn't listening or even paying attention until it was too late. Everyone was too busy getting on with their lives, struggling for survival as they paid taxes to support their continued low-level existence.

'And what would *you* do to win public confidence, Bernice?'

'Be honest. Tell them mistakes were made. That you've heard their demands. That you've learned the lessons you needed to learn. That

COVID is unprecedented in living memory. Then offer them a strategy that really is designed to fix the NHS and COVID situations together.'

Fooling the public is an art form that requires an excellent memory to avoid detection. His party had been lying about the NHS for more than ten years now. Privatisation was well established but still had some way to go before the entire medical industry could be fully converted. Maintaining the façade had arguably proven more challenging than he'd anticipated. The medical staff were clearly well aware of what was going on around them. Yet, they only partly understood why they had not gotten any pay rises. The government hoped they would seek employment elsewhere and continue to leave. That way, the NHS would always be under-resourced and ill-equipped to deal with a growing population of elderly and sick. The need for privatisation in more sectors would then emerge. It was a straightforward strategy that had been devised ages ago. At this point, to do anything that might be viewed as genuinely helpful to the NHS would be taken as an affront to the efforts of countless party predecessors. For that reason, he needed to think carefully before committing to the public anything that could later be used against him. Yet, he knew Bernice was right. The public did need something to bring them together, and little would work better than the NHS.

'Thank you, Bernice. That will be all for now.'

Alone now, Streaker sat pondering over what had to be. It would probably make him the most famous prime minister in history – a man who had taken a calculated risk and won. Losing not an option. Losing was for losers, not winners. There was bound to be an enormous hum of complaints. His party would not understand his strategy. This was a necessity, however. It needed to appear real, had to evoke passion. It was when people spoke with passion that they were at their most powerful. He needed that power, needed the public to witness it, needed the media to report it, needed the private companies to fear it. He had an idea.

A call to Bandip now, and they would begin.

*****

'Let me get this straight, Rupert. You want us to start a war with the island of Huvva in the Pacific and blame it on Somalian pirates. You know that Huvva is nowhere near Somalia, right?'

'It doesn't matter where it is. No one will be paying attention.'

'Except the navy', Bandip replied dryly.

'If we don't do this, there's every possibility that we'll lose the next general election.'

'It's very extreme, Rupert, and totally illegal', he argued. 'Should you ever be found out, you'll end up in the Tower.'

'Enough with the negative speculations, Jonathon. Can *you* arrange it or do I need to hire a new fixer?'

'I was merely pointing out potential problems. Of course, I can fix it', he sniffed. 'I just need to find a local chum in the region first.'

CHAPTER 2

Cabinet Meeting – for the good of the country

Cabinet meetings were never rushed affairs. The off-white room prepared for the 10:00 meeting was naturally light and airy because of its large floor-to-ceiling windows. Three brass chandeliers hung from the ceiling high above.

Twenty-two ministers gathered around a magnificent boat-shaped table purchased during the Gladstone era. It was covered in a green cloth of exquisite texture that dangled close to the sturdy legs of the table, made of the finest oak. The chairs around it were solid mahogany, also dating back to Gladstone. It was the epitome of British manufacturing. Only the prime minister's seat, placed In front of the marble fireplace, had with arms easy that made it easy to recognise. The decor of the cabinet room was a lesson in less appearing to be more. A solitary portrait of Sir Robert Walpole by Jean Baptiste van Loo hung over the fireplace – the only display of a globally significant history. The ministers' appointment as members of Her Majesty's Most Honourable Privy Council allowed them the use of term 'The Right Honourable', while their seating arrangement at the table reflected their seniority.

As Streaker entered the room, the ministers collectively held their breath. The news headlines were continuing to claim that Allfores and Streaker were lovers who enjoyed being watched by friends while having sex in church settings. Concerns over their moral and religious values were growing. However, Bandip had not been slow in challenging those claims by having a rival newspaper issue a statement from Number 10, denying the validity of the photograph and insisting instead that it was a Photoshop mock-up – something that could be proved. He had also contacted Jeffrey Craftee, Streaker's solicitor, to begin libel proceedings.

'I've had better mornings', Streaker confessed with a wry smile. 'But I can categorically deny whatever you've read about me and Kate Allfores. Jonathon is instructing my solicitor to initiate libel proceedings against the newspaper as we speak. There is concrete evidence to prove quite clearly that the photograph is fake. At least my part in it.'

'What about Allfores?' asked Martin Probe, the secretary of state for housing.

'She was clearly involved in such antics during her younger years. Unfortunately, that kind of behaviour is unacceptable even in today's liberal environment. However, she has indeed proved quite useful in her current post and will be moved to a less public role. Now if that's all, I'd like to get on with the real reasons we're all here. To manage this country that is.' The murmur of agreement from everyone was enough to show that he had dodged another silver bullet. 'Good. What's happening on the COVID front?'

The health minister, Terence Remedy, looked up, slightly dazed from one too many sleepless night. 'We're issuing another round of recommendations for the public to follow should new spikes be identified. A copy of the recommendations has been arranged for everyone here.'

'How are you holding up, Terence? You look a trifle weary. You haven't caught that blasted virus yourself, have you?' Streaker's concern for a colleague was quite unprecedented.

'No, I'm clear. I took a test this morning. I'm tired, that's all. I'm fine, thank you for asking.'

'We wouldn't want you to have a break-down now.' Streaker's tone suggested genuine concern.

'Thanks again, Prime Minister.'

'Not at all, Terence.' Streaker wore a sympathetic smile, hiding his uncertainty over who could be available to replace the incumbent health minister. The biggest problem was that no one wanted the job. Most saw it as a career graveyard. Bandip figured that a Black female replacement would be preferable. The only trouble was that no

Black women were currently available. Not that that was really an insurmountable problem; one could always be imported from elsewhere for the right amount of money.

'I think it's clear that the public acknowledge this to be an extraordinary situation. They've witnessed the implementation of our furlough scheme to help them and what not. However, we need to do more to maintain a certain level of confidence that seems to waver with each headline. I want to see consistency. We need it. The public needs it. So, has anyone got ideas about how we might go about getting it?'

Silence. Twenty-one ministers had the same black stares on their faces, each wishing someone else would suggest something, anything. Basil Dence was the first to speak.

'I think…'

That would be a first, Streaker thought. The rich, entitled transport minister was only present there because of family influence. The prime minister's family too had supported his own rise to power. Some called Dence's presence karma. Creating a challenge that those with influential families expected to be accepted without a second thought.

'We need to distract the public', he beamed, delighted at having all the attention on himself.

Good, but where is this going? Streaker shifted uneasily in anticipation, recalling that Dence was responsible for an attempt to introduce camel taxis for ministers, with camels having precedents over all other vehicles on the road. He extolled their virtues: less pollution and cheaper than running a limousine. Additionally, the installation of stables at Westminster offered fresh employment, as did training and maintaining the camel drivers. Collecting the camel droppings also necessitated a fresh intake of highway maintenance workers. Streaker admitted later that he hadn't seen it coming. Being blindsided by one of his ministers had not won Dence any brownie points. From that point on, Streaker had ordered Bandip to closely monitor him.

'I suggest that we help employees reach their workplaces in environmentally friendly ways.'

He's at it again. Streaker stiffened. Bandip would need to work another miracle to keep Streaker from losing the support of the Dence family.

'I suggest that we use the Thames as a way of avoiding clogging up roads and also reducing emissions. It really would be a win for us.'

'You're suggesting river ferries?' Streaker queried. This was not new, and there were already ferries operating on the river. Reluctantly, he further asked, 'How is your idea any different from what is already there on the river?'

'Long boats, Prime Minister.' He said it as though he expected Streaker's eyes ti light up like a bulb at his reply.

'I'm still not following you, Basil?'

'I'm suggesting that we get our small boat builders to construct a thousand long boats. Like the ones that were used by the Vikings. They would make for a really fun way to ferry people up and down the river. They'll be capable of accommodating fifty passengers and crew. Apart from the novelty, it would definitely detract from the whole COVID thing.'

Setting us back several hundred years, hmmm, Streaker thought. He could easily imagine the media storm that would follow. 'But weren't Viking long boats crewed by oarsmen?'

'That's the beauty of my idea, Prime Minister. No foul toxic fumes.' Dence looked positively pleased with himself, grinning inanely at the sea of confused faces around him.

'How many oarsmen does it take to man one of these things?'

'There can be as many as sixty in really big ones, but I'm suggesting boats powered by twenty-four oars.'

The health minister was the next to ask, 'But where would you find enough people to man a thousand long boats? I mean you're talking about twenty-four thousand oarsmen. How much would you suggest we pay them to row up and down the river?'

'Nothing.'

Streaker couldn't resist engaging, 'Nothing?' Had Dence finally discovered a solution that was economically sound?

'We use prison inmates.'

It is incredible, Streaker thought to himself. Dence had gone to public school. He knew that for certain because they had been in the same class. 'You're suggesting that we use twenty-four thousand prison inmates to row a thousand long boats up and down the river for people to go to and from work? Do you expect the public to pay for these journeys?'

'A nominal amount. Perhaps a pound. Their being so cheap will have the public knocked out travelling into the heart of London.' Dence studied the serious expressions of the other cabinet members. None flinched; not a single one expressed what they were thinking. He had expected them to appear elated at his suggestion at the very least. Less grim-faced, definitely.

The home secretary Felicity Hangready said, 'You do realise that slavery is illegal in the UK?'

Silence. Watching Dence deflate was like looking at a tortured mushroom implode.

'Additionally, the cost of a squad large enough to prevent a mutiny on the river for each boat would probably prove financially prohibitive.'

'Are you done, Basil?' Streaker asked and received a nod in response. 'Has anyone else got any credible suggestions to help win over the public confidence by showing them we know what we're doing?' Streaker tried to avoid looking at the pathetic disappointment on Dence's face.

'We might try getting the PPE right', a small voice answered from his left.

He turned his gaze on Monica Moon. The minister without a portfolio appeared nervous under his scrutiny. A thin, forty-something brunette with sharp green eyes, Streaker often spotted her wandering around Westminster and Number 10, as though she were lost. Perhaps it was time he gave her a proper job. 'You were saying, Monica?'

'There are still hospitals that are complaining about how don't have enough PPE. If there's a second or third wave of the virus infection, the public will feel reassured to learn that we've got enough PPE in our contingency to last us a year at least.'

'Sounds expensive', he remarked, turning to the health minister.

'It would be. Currently, we're following a mobile support PPE service for all hospitals in England and Wales where we have a central store that distributes on demand. It makes it easier to cater to those regions that have spikes while monitoring the ones that don't. It's a cost-saving exercise.'

'And how much PPE do we have if everything goes tits up?'

'Enough for six weeks.'

'Better double it', Streaker said.

'We were going to use what we saved on PPE to employ agency staff. That would mean cutting their number by about a fifth. That would leave the NHS without a large slice of physical resources that they need in order to avoid being swamped.'

'That's fine. It puts more pressure on the NHS and demonstrates yet again that it can't cope without outside help, boosting our plans for privatisation. In addition, I've been considering the major move of establishing an American-funded COVID response centre that would supplement what the NHS has on offer. Of course, anyone using the American scheme would have to pay, but it could lighten the load on the NHS and be viewed by the public as a necessary step to overcome shortages in hospitals.'

'That sounds like a great idea', the health minister said. This was the first time he had heard it, and it had caught his colleagues as well as him by surprise. 'My only concern is that the left will use it to highlight an American intention to challenge the NHS. People are frightened of privatisation and this country mirroring the US in terms of losing a medical facility with all capability, theoretically at least.'

'It will', Streaker said. 'But staff at the American centre will be highly paid compared to those employed by the NHS. Once the Americans have set-up the first centre, others will follow right across the country. We'll see a mass exodus of staff joining them. Nothing speaks louder than being well paid, as we all know.' It had been one of Streaker's secrets. Something he had negotiated with his American counterpart. Keeping it to himself until now had been a necessity. The cabinet had a leak, he knew; someone around him willing to betray his trust. It was nothing more than a demonstration of contempt. Yet, they were too cowardly to show themselves. It crossed his mind that it could be the same weasel who had handed the evening paper a photo of him and Allfores. In fact, it was highly likely that they were one and the same. Finding the traitorous cur was now a personal priority. Contacting Beattie

Beaver, an American newspaper baron with his empire, not including the evening newspaper, had not helped. However, discovering who was feeding information to one of his rivals gave him the type of challenge he enjoyed. He pledged to find the culprit and get back to him. Streaker had no reason to disbelieve that. Beattie didn't know failure. A totally ruthless man, his empire had grown without showing any sign of mercy towards the opposition. There were no rules in his world. Dog ate dog or died. Kicking a downed rival ensured a win with no possibility of a retaliatory fight. Streaker admired him and often himself wished to be as ruthless, but the public would quickly make a fuss if he were. The games he played were, at times, much more cunning – how he liked it. He didn't doubt that news about an American COVID response centre would be leaked. When it was, Beattie would be ready. 'That was my piece of good news. What about illegal immigrants, Home Secretary?'

His formal sounding question caught everyone's attention. Was Streaker angry with the home secretary? Not using a minister's first name was usually an indication.

The home secretary replied in an equally formal manner, which generated its own uncertainty and tension. 'We've had a drop in illegal immigrant arrests. In March this year, it went down by nine hundred or thereabouts. The number currently in detention is around twelve hundred. The cost per night per detainee is around a hundred pounds, totalling at an annual cost of one hundred and twenty thousand pounds for their bed space. This is a low-cost figure that can be expended without being bashed by the media over illegal immigrant costs. Just remember, it doesn't include security, transport, or administration charges, which would expose just how incredibly expensive it is.'

'What percentage are we returning?' Streaker asked.

'Enforced returns for both EU nationals and non-EU nationals are down. EU nationals have accounted for about forty percent of those returned, split between Romanian and Polish nationals, which accounted for more than fifty five percent of EU returned nationals. The number of returned non-EU citizens saw a drop of around thirty percent.'

'Sounds like we're doing well', said Streaker.

'Thank you, Prime Minister', the home secretary replied before her tone hardened. 'There is another matter to which I'd like to draw to the cabinet's attention.'

'Very well', the prime minister said, as if bored at the very thought of another issue from her.

'It's this business of you wanting an earpiece when attending PMQs. The Commons speaker is currently refusing to agree, citing national security. It is possible one of your advisors might let slip something that could be picked up by the media. She thinks it too risky.'

Streaker had asked her to intervene on his behalf even though she had stubbornly disagreed with the idea, recognising problems without having them spelled out to her by the Commons speaker. As home secretary, she felt she appeared foolish in attempting to ignore the law she was meant to enforce. It had caused an argument between her and Streaker, with him pushing back by reminding her that he was her boss.

'What about cutting back on the social distancing rules?'

'She won't budge on that either. Says she can't see any reason why the guidelines for the public should not also be followed by parliament. Her argument is that we're meant to be role models. I did warn you.'

Streaker frowned, irritated that he had remained vulnerable at question time, unable to receive prompts from his private secretaries who usually sat directly behind him. It was becoming increasingly difficult to evade awkward questions from his primary adversary, Rex Pounding. So much so that it was making him desperate for support from his advisors. Without it, there was a real possibility that his floundering responses could lose him public support. Once cracks began to appear in his public image, it was a slippery slope to it being shattered. 'That's absolutely no help whatsoever. How the hell am I meant to stop taking a public pounding from Pounding?'

'Try being honest', Monica Moon uttered the words to a startled room.

Streaker frowned so deeply that his eyebrows almost became joined at the nose. 'Are you insane!'

'May I speak freely, Prime Minister?'

'You don't appear to have had a problem doing that till now. Get on with it!'

'I've been studying your counterpart in the U.S. By telling people what he's really doing, he's been getting away with doing it. The public, well a percentage of them, support him. They like the idea of a leader doing what he says. Even when it trashes their Constitution. No one understands the reasons, which must be complex, but I feel like you might as well try the same.'

She was correct. Streaker had watched his idol with admiration, taking on all his opponents and never once giving in to honesty, integrity, and scruples. He flouted age-old traditions that hinged on long-extolled values, facing down the opposition while appearing to be getting away with it.

'It's a dangerous strategy. One only a desperate individual would adopt. Are you really desperate, Prime Minister?' Featherlight, the minister for Northern Ireland, asked. The room silent in anticipation.

'What do you say Moon, am I desperate?'

'If you're not', she said in a small, inconsequential voice that disguised a depth of strategic thinking that he was beginning to appreciate, 'then you should be, Prime Minister. You have a credible opponent in Rex Pounding, and the public is taking note of what he says, something that couldn't be said of his predecessor. Don't make the mistake of believing that honesty can't get you what you want. Think like the Americans.'

The Americans had proven that being blatant about their intentions was possible. Definitely lie when denying the ultimate intention. Call it law and order. National security. Bring in the fear factor by suggesting what might happen if Draconian measures were not implemented in the community. Use a common enemy that did not separate parts of the community by race. Criminal behaviour common to all. People wouldn't want to live with the worry that they were going to be attacked in their homes. And unless law and order were maintained, it could happen. Just the fact that it could happen was enough to spark public support. 'You realise how that would be a complete change of tack? Additionally, the British aren't as volatile as the Americans. It takes a lot more to get them going.'

'Not really, Prime Minister', Moon replied. The room couldn't have been more hushed. No one dared to challenge the prime minister and survived.

'Explain yourself, Monica', he said, still referring to her by her first name. A good sign.

'The last major riots occurred in 2017, outside Forest Gate police station, after the death of a suspect at the time of his arrest. The riots were short-lived because police action was supported by a majority of the public. Law and order was restored. It was the same in 2011 when a police shooting killed a suspect in Tottenham. Law and order was once again restored because a majority of the public wanted it. In June this year, the police were forced to flee a mini riot because they were outnumbered. The public was outraged that such a thing could happen. They have shown that they will support law and order no matter when necessary, irrespective of the cost to their freedoms. The point I'm making, Prime Minister, is that you have an opportunity to achieve enormous political and social gains and meet the party's political agenda by simply taking the reins like your American counterpart and shaking out the cobwebs. Get rid of the old guard in the Civil Service. Then you'll be free. Simply tell the public, within reason, what your intentions are.

They'll follow strong leadership as they did with Winston Churchill.'

'Winston Churchill was facing a visible threat as the allied nations were being invaded', Featherlight pointed out.

'COVID is a war that demands decisive and difficult actions from the government if It's to be defeated. Winning means the survival of a maximum number of people before a vaccination is finally found.' Moon's small inconsequential voice had gained strength. It was now without a perceptible murmur of timidity. 'Explain the war to the public. Don't simply state that we're at war with a virus. Tell them what needs to be achieved. It hasn't been done in such a basic form, but it needs to be done if we're to survive another lock-down. Don't leave it to the public's imagination.'

'Whoa, who said anything about a second lock-down?' Featherlight butted in.

'There's every reason to believe that a second wave will hit and that it will be greater than the first. Allowing people to mingle even at a distance was bound to make that happen, but it couldn't really be helped. We need to use what the science tells us now. Start preparing the public and get them into fear mode. They're far more malleable that way. While they're worrying over COVID, you can bring in whatever policies you deem fit. Doing so honestly will give you the upper hand, and Rex Pounding will be lost in the noise of your advances.'

Streaker was impressed. The thin brunette with sharp green eyes was much more than what his first impressions of her suggested. 'What you're suggesting is that we increase our repertoire when it comes to COVID now rather than later. Pounding won't be able to argue with that. He wouldn't dare. Then, as the public is back under lock-down, you expect us to introduce Draconian measures to keep them there, at the same time introducing far-reaching policies likely to be challenged by our rivals. There we'll win because we have the numbers in the House. All of it would have done blatantly so that no one could suggest that we misled the public.'

'That's precisely what I'm suggesting, Prime Minister.'

'How badly will that impact the economy, Raif?'

Raif Moolah, the chancellor of the exchequer sighed. 'Well, we always knew there'd be a possibility of a second lock-down. I did build in a contingency if it were to happen. However, much will depend on who we limit to outside employment.'

'Raif, can we keep the economy moving under lock down?' Streaker asked. 'That's what we need to know.'

'Only if we accept that there will be losses, possibly significant ones.'

'Before you say that we need to make tough decisions, I need something better in order to suppress public anger.'

Moon raised her hand, as if in class. 'If I might suggest something, Prime Minister.'

'Certainly, Monica. You appear to be the only one here with any credible ideas.'

'Actually, a thought just occurred to me, Prime Minister', Dence interrupted.

'Keep it to yourself!' Streaker barked. 'Please continue, Monica.'

'You should offer your resignation', she said.

Everyone sat up. Everyone except Streaker that is. 'What would be the point of that?'

'Your popularity is on the wane. It might be a temporary hiccup, or it might be a warning of impending doom. COVID hasn't done this government any favours whatsoever. So, you should admit that there have been mistakes, give them what they want to hear.'

'Which is?'

'Ask for their forgiveness so you can use what you've learned from the mistakes to continue to do your best in defending them against the virus. Suggest that if they no longer believe in you then you will offer your resignation and stand down as prime minister for someone else from the party to take over.'

'You want me to call for a referendum?'

'Definitely not', she dismissed the idea without hesitation. 'My guess is that you'll find public opinion swayed in your favour after the transmission. People like to see their leader eat humble pie when necessary. It makes you more relatable to them.'

His eyes were narrowed so tight that they were just slits. 'It seems too easy.'

'I'm certain you'll be seen as a hero. Any leader who admits to being fallible deserves a second chance. Right now, you remain our best hope to get Brexit done and to lead us out of this dire situation with the virus.'

'Pounding might try going for a general election if I offer my resignation', he said.

'He might, but we're talking about a change in the party's leadership, not the government. You took over from an incumbent prime minister. There's no reason for that to change at this stage.'

Streaker sucked in a deep breath. 'Eating humble pie. Just might work. I like it Monica.'

She would not have smiled more brightly if he had handed her a million pounds. Her shoulders rose a half inch from their more natural slump, and her spine straightened, lifting her head, so that she now appeared the equal of those around her.

'I'd like you to take the lead on this, Monica. Anything you need, just ask.'

'Yes, Prime Minister. Thank you.'

'Okay, what's next on the agenda?'

'The number of deaths due to coronavirus remains the highest in Europe. It really make us look bad', Hangready said. 'I was wondering if we might be able to tweak the figures to reduce the number of deaths?'

'I don't see how', Remedy replied. 'The number of people dying from the virus is incredibly high, and I'm not sure how the figures could be tweaked to reduce them?'

'I heard that someone having the virus was run down by a bus and killed but the death was still recorded as a virus death. Surely, we can identify the number of people dying from other reasons even though they have the virus. We should be recording those deaths separately. I mean, what about cancer patients? None of those deaths should be recorded as virus deaths even if they have it and die from it. Doing so will reduce the death rate figures, which will help us not look as bad as we do.'

'Unfortunately, not everyone with the virus gets run down by a bus', Remedy argued. 'Also, the number of cancer patients with COVID is not high enough to make a big difference in the stats.'

'Small steps', Hangready said. 'Start collecting information on what else could be wrong with the people that have died from the virus. Having any other diseases or ailments should mean that they are recorded as dying from that rather than COVID', she replied firmly.

'You're suggesting that we blame alternative ailments for the high death rate?' he asked, seeking clarity.

'I'm suggesting that we employ a strategy that gets us out of this shit!" she snapped irritably. 'Don't you agree, Rupert?'

'If we can reduce the death rate figures relating to COVID, we must. I don't like taking bottom place to the rest of Europe.'

'I'll see what's possible', Remedy replied. The problem was not as easy as Hangready made it sound. Families would have been told that their relatives had died from COVID. Not that they had to be told anything different unless they made enquiries to check. If that were to happen, however, things could become awkward. He sighed, hopeful that no one would check.

'Now is there anything else requiring our attention?'

'Just a minor point, Prime Minister', Sir Sid Mid, chief secretary to the Treasury, said with hand raised to catch Streaker's eye. He was a soft-spoken man, unaccustomed to raising his voice above a low decibel point, sensitive to his own hearing. 'I've been learning of the growing concern that too many CEOs are receiving huge pay-offs before walking away as their companies fail and staff are made redundant. I'm afraid the media is working overtime to expose a situation that can only get worse as COVID damage to the economy becomes clearer. There's a desperate need to justify the reasons high-end management receive such huge rewards as their companies, and their workers, fall into dark times together.'

'You're not suggesting they shouldn't be handed these lavish pay-outs, are you Sid?'

The other man appeared horrified. 'Of course not, Prime Minister! Not at all. What I'm suggesting is that we establish a new argument that can be considered as reasonable justification in most cases. You might consider it a fresh threshold to stifle dissonance or at least lock it into a circle of argument without answer. People need to be paid for the status they've achieved, prime minister. It's not a CEO's responsibility if their company goes down the drain. They will undoubtedly have done their best.'

'Quite right', Streaker agreed. 'I appreciate the point you make. It's unthinkable that a CEO should walk away from a multi-million-pound company with just a bit of cash before it sinks into oblivion. Of course, convincing the workforce and the public of a need for this tradition to continue will be hard, but I do not suppose it is impossible. I'll ask Jonathon Bandip to give it some consideration. I'm sure the right words can be found.'

'Perhaps we ought to consider better help for the workers in such situations?' Dence added.

Streaker closed his eyes to contain a surge of anger. 'Are you suggesting that we aren't considering them already, Basil?'

'No, of course not, Prime Minister. What I'm suggesting is that we might try doing more for them to placate bad feelings as their CEO walks away with millions while they're out of work and vulnerable.'

'Do that just once, and you'll set a costly precedent. Taking care of the vulnerable is not how this government operates. You should know that by now, Basil!'

'Yes, Prime Minister.'

***

The next day, the newspapers were filled with reports of the government's intention to allow an American medical centre to be sited in London as a help to cope with the COVID pandemic. The expected leak occurred, and, on this occasion, Streaker was not disappointed.

CHAPTER THREE

The cost of an extra-marital relationship

The growth in the numbers seeking independence in Wales was a sign of the times. Streaker dropped the latest report on his desk, irritated at how yet another part of the UK wanted to break free from Westminster. Some simply didn't know when they were well off. Wales wouldn't be able to sustain its standard of living were it to actually separate from the UK – much like Scotland or Northern Ireland. Why didn't that stop the calls for independence? Were they suggesting that rule by Westminster was worse than a drop in their standard of living?

Scottish ministers claimed that Scotland had been subsidising the UK over the past 32 years. Statistics! What they don't voice is the loss of access to the NHS, lower pensions, and higher taxation. Additionally, issuing new currency would cost a small fortune.

However, supporters of independence for the three other countries in the union had been working hard to resolve the arguments that had previously scuppered Scotland's last attempt at it, including a new currency for the three countries. By linking this new currency to a collection of different currencies, stability was possible. For practical reasons though, the new currency would be weighted towards the Sterling and the Euro. This would alleviate how the surges and fluctuations in England or Europe could impact it.

What continued to perplex him was what the other three countries would do if they were actually granted independence. Would they wish to remain independent or join the

Europeans? Joining Europe would remove the power they had recovered from Westminster. Passing it on to Brussels appeared odd under the circumstances, as the EU was more an autocracy than a democracy. Joining the Eu would only leave them less capable of arguing for themselves against the demands of other larger countries. Was that how the countries' public saw the argument for independence? He doubted it.

Bandip joined him, seating himself opposite the prime minister. Noting Streaker's agitated expression, he tried make him comfortable. 'There's someone here to see you.'

'I haven't got any meetings now.'

'It's Bernard Allfores. Kate Allfores' husband.'

'What's he doing here?' The prospect of having to face down with a jealous husband, brushing everything else aside, at this time seemed ridiculous. 'Tell him I'm out.'

'He knows you're in', Bandip replied.

'Damn, I thought you were meant to shield me from unwanted visitors.'

'If he's turned away, there's a possibility he'll go to the press. I think it is necessary that you speak with him. For Jessica's sake.'

'What are you talking about?' Streaker appeared confused. Having a conversation with an irate husband whose wife he had shagged silly was not a prospect he cared to entertain. 'Is he armed?'

'He's fine.' Then he quickly corrected himself, 'Well, not fine; just needs to talk.'

'What does he know?'

'I'd say he knows everything.'

'You mean including our most recent encounter?' Streaker asked. His genuine concern was evident on his pasty features.

'I believe so.' Bandip was cool, calm, and composed. This was why he had been hired as a fixer. He always knew best. 'You need to trust me with this.'

'What do you think he intends to do?'

'Nothing physical. Not at this point. My guess is that he'll try to blackmail you.'

'Blackmail!'

'We moved his wife to a less important position, remember? To a basement somewhere. My guess is he wants her out of there. She didn't go willingly. I thought she could make a fuss. This might be it.'

'Blast. I never imagined Kate to be a squealer.'

'Having her backside on full view to the nation tends to do that, especially when her husband isn't the one behind it.'

'If Jessica comes home and finds Allfores here, she's going to know something's up. She can smell a rat from a hundred yards away. One look at him, and she'll know that I lied. I really can't afford that.'

'Then I suggest you deal with him as quickly as possible so that he leaves before Jessica gets home.'

Streaker rose from the seat and stood by the window as Bandip slipped out of the room. Moments later, Bernard Allfores joined him. Allfores was a tall, broad-shouldered man who looked fit and capable. A broken nose suggested that he was not unaccustomed to fighting for what he wanted.

'I know everything', he said, skipping any introduction.

'What is it that you want?' Streaker asked in a matter-of-fact fashion.

'Promotion for me', he said.

'Where do you work?'

'At the Office for National Statistics.'

'What grade?'

'Senior executive officer.'

'Fine. I'll see that you're promoted to deputy assistant director.'

'Assistant under secretary. Nothing less.'

'Where were you educated?' Streaker asked, vaguely recalling something Kate had told him. Her family had been unhappy that she had married someone beneath her, an ordinary member of the public.

'I'm not here for a job interview, you wife shagger!'

'I still need to know where you were educated. Which university?'

'The university of London!' he replied angrily.

'Oh dear.' Streaker felt a chill go over him. Allfores wasn't part of the Establishment. It didn't matter how good he was at his job; he would remain an outsider – someone who wouldn't understand or appreciate the complexities of how the Establishment managed the country. 'I can't do it. Someone will complain.'

'That's the price you pay for shagging my wife!' His face looked angrier than before. His hands were clasped by his sides, his fists tight bunches of muscle and bone.

A rush of concern made Streaker reconsider. There was no room for negotiation. Agreeing to Allfores' demand was all he could do. He didn't like it. He wasn't meant to like it. That was the point of blackmail. It would cause him trouble. He wondered what Kate wanted. 'What about her?'

'You can leave her where you put her. She deserves it. Just make sure I'm promoted within the month. Otherwise, I'll call your wife and the press.' As he watched the prime minister squirm, his hands unclasped. He was satisfied. Turning without looking back, he left the room, the door ajar behind him.

Bandip returned as soon as he was gone, 'Well?'

'He studied at the University of London but wants a two-step promotion', he said bitterly. 'I had to agree. Didn't have a choice.'

'What about Kate?'

'She stays where she is. Apparently, it's her penalty for straying away from home.'

'It's a small price. He could have demanded more.'

'Maybe you should call him back!' Streaker dropped into the seat with a huff. 'I was just looking at the independence papers for Scotland and the others when he showed up. As if Rob Roy being alive and well wasn't bad enough, I've just been squeezed by one of the cast of East Enders for a top-level government job.'

'You're doing very well, Rupert. Jessica won't know the truth. Your family is safe.'

'Women are so demanding. They don't know how hard it is to resist keeping it in a bloke's trousers when the opportunity presents itself.'

'And now there's no need for her to ever know.'

'Just promise me that if I ever get another opportunity to do it, you'll ensure it doesn't happen. I don't think I can live through a repeat of this.'

'I don't think you need concern yourself about coming across Allfores any time soon. I found her a wonderful underground post working for the ministry of defence, for the nuclear fallout shelter program.'

'I didn't know we still had a program dealing with that.'

'We don't, Rupert. It's her job to sketch up a draft covering the possibility for the entire country. Should take her about three or four years at least.'

Streaker's face lit up. 'Splendid, Jonathon! And what about these idiots wanting their Independence Day?'

'Mmmh, an alliance by the other three countries does present a bit of a problem.'

'What's up with these people? They get testy about being ripped off by us, but it's okay for the EU to do it? Just doesn't make sense to me.'

'If only it were that simple, Rupert. We could flush it down the toilet in a matter of days. Unfortunately, my spies tell me they intend on remaining an independent alliance that is capable of making deals as a group with whoever they wish. Without England, they would be looked on more favourably, while we would be seen as *Billy No Mates*.'

'We'd still have the largest population. Trade deals with us would still be necessary for them to survive.'

'Of course, but their plan entails a recall of all their nationals living in England.'

'You seem to know a lot about their plan.'

'I've been hearing rumblings for some time, so I put people in place before things became too difficult', he casually remarked, knowing Streaker would be pleased. 'Our real concern is that Ireland could feel threatened by their alliance and might opt to join it even on Northern Irish terms. Doing so would make their alliance even stronger.'

'Bloody hell! The Queen really will be pissed, and on my watch!'

'It will never happen', Bandip suddenly said. 'September 2014 isn't a forgotten memory. The Scots voted to remain part of the UK for valid reasons. Money is key. If the people believe they will be worse off, they won't want anything to do with it.'

'Then, we need to ensure that it is precisely what they believe. We can't allow an alliance to put us on the backfoot. Next thing you know, they'll consider themselves our equals. It would be a disaster. Do whatever it takes to scupper this.'

'What about Allfores, Rupert? If you give him that promotion, then what's to prevent him from wanting another at some point in the future? Also, what if he has a few other chums that he wants promoted? You could be leaving yourself open to further abuse by him and others. And all from the wrong side of the tracks, Rupert. It would be a hard pill for our circle to swallow.'

Streaker scratched his head at the troubling thought.

***

The Scottish first minister Bonnie Burns looked sombre as Streaker led her into his office. The urgent meeting called by him did not come to her as a complete surprise. But his insistence that it be held in London rather than Scotland, or that they speak without advisors present, did. He wasn't certain doing so would intimidate her but hoped it would allow her to speak more freely. His plan was a straightforward one: dissuade her from continuing with the alliance.

'I wanted to see you alone so that we could speak freely.'

'Of course,' she replied demurely. In her late forties, Burns had inherited the red hair and alabaster complexion of her ancestors, while her confident dark-brown eyes held his gaze. Although not traditionally beautiful, she was, however, markedly attractive and had caught his attention on more than one occasion as possible conquest material. Another notch on his gun. Not that she hadn't noticed his attention or compartmentalised it for the right opportunity.

'Your intention to form an alliance with Wales and Northern Ireland is unnecessary', he began.

'It has you worried', she retorted.

'Only in as much as it will prove to be a waste of money. Something neither of us can afford. That's why, `I wanted to take this opportunity to speak with you. There must be something that

I can offer to keep you from going down the same road we travelled in 2014.'

'Six years is a long time, Rupert. The world has moved on. COVID has changed everything. Scotland is not the same as it was six years ago. The UK is no longer a part of the EU. The people who were unable to vote back then can. Also, your government has been in power since 2010 – an entire decade – and the country feels like it's gone backwards.'

'You think you will be able to re-join the EU by forming an alliance, is that it?'

'It's an option that will be back on the table if we wish. Unlike if we remain with England.'

'England is still your biggest trading partner and will be for the foreseeable future. So, why make it tough for both of us by getting a divorce?'

'We don't want to be ruled by you any longer. We both know that Scotland can do very well on its own.'

'I don't agree', he blustered. 'Scotland has done well because it is a part of the UK. Break that connect, and you'll jeopardise both our futures.'

'That's rubbish, and you know it. You're living in the past, Rupert, your colonial past. It's time you caught up with the rest of us. The public has grown more sophisticated, and common sense is seen as a skill equivalent to an academic qualification. The Establishment has abused the common sense of the Scottish people as well as its own for far too long. You've brought this on yourselves. No one wants to be looked down on because they weren't born with a silver spoon. That's the old-world Scotland intends to escape. It's your world, Rupert.'

'What are you on about, Bonnie? No one looks down on the Scots. Some of my best friends are from Scotland.'

'That doesn't mean you see them as equals, Rupert.'

'What can I offer you, so you stop seeking independence?' he bluntly asked.

'Independence', she grinned. 'There is nothing other than that. If all you were going to offer was a stream of things I don't want, we could have done this over the phone.'

'I want to keep the union together, Bonnie. We're stronger together. The Queen wants it too.'

'Not my problem. I represent the Scottish people. A strong Scotland is all I care about. You took us out of the EU.

You couldn't be stronger now than you were as a member of the EU. If that couldn't keep England, why should your argument convince me that remaining in the UK makes Scotland stronger? We believe the rest of the UK is a drain on our people. We'd be richer without you.'

'Only by maintaining the status quo but leaving England will change everything. We'll be forced to rebuild our trading relationship with border controls tariffs. You know the form. Your people will require passports and visas to enter our land. Do you really want that?'

'We don't like being ruled by Westminster or the Crown. It's outdated. The Scottish people need to feel that they're in command of their own destinies, as do the Welsh and the Northern Irish. You above all else should understand that since you claim it was part of the reason you wanted out of the EU.'

'The EU is an autocracy just a step below despotism. There's too much corruption for a single nation to alleviate or even mould into something better. The UK was losing money hand over fist no matter what the federalists claim. We all knew it, but helping the poorer countries was necessary to improve their low standard of living. The lie was that we could do so while maintaining our own standard of living.'

'What you say is true, but it also represents why Scotland needs to divorce England.'

'Do you not think that Wales and Northern Ireland will cost Scotland even more than England does? Northern Ireland in particular has an inadequate infrastructure by our standards. It will take years before its capable of maintaining its population without English support or rather Scottish support if I may. The cost will be punishing.'

'You paint a dark picture, Rupert. As always.'

'It's an honest picture, Bonnie.'

'It's your version of honesty, Rupert. Not mine.'

'There must be something. Some way we can find a mutually agreeable arrangement without Scotland splitting from the UK?'

'Why didn't you ask for representatives from the other two?'

'Because it's you who leads them. Whatever you agree on, they'll follow. They're sheep; you're a ram.'

'And I'm for independence.'

'Damn it, Bonnie. There must be something I can say or do that will sway you away from this ridiculously destructive course of action.'

She rose from her seat. 'There really was extraordinarily little for us to talk about. I won't be returning for another of these little get-togethers, Rupert. At least not until after the next referendum in 2021.'

Leaving without turning back, she closed the door behind her. The isolation of his office suddenly, and for the first time, began to make him uncomfortable. It was where he had wished to be as a child. All the people he had ever admired had been here, had struggled with their own obstacles and overcome them. Now it was his turn. He could not let his predecessors down. He would not. He had to find a crack in her armour, a tiny chink in which he could sew enough spin to destroy everything that Bonnie Burns dreamed about. Losing a second referendum for independence would seal her doom and lay to bed any thoughts of attempting a third referendum for the next twenty years. Keeping the Union united now his God-given priority.

***

Donna Davies, the first minister of Wales, unhesitatingly accepted the invitation to meet with Streaker at Number 10. Bonnie Burns had warned her that an invitation was in the offing and what it was that the prime minister wanted to discuss. No surprise there. Nor the fact that their secret intention had been leaked to him. Streaker and Bandip were infamous for having 'ears' throughout the realm.

'Nice of you to come at such short notice, Donna', he began as she made herself comfortable at the small coffee table by the fireplace in his office.

Another modern, middle-aged woman –
Smart, attractive, and vivacious.
Everything required to stir Streaker's
inner animal.

'It took me by surprise, Rupert. I
hope there's not more bad news related
to COVID?'

She knew the reason for her visit
– of that he was certain. She was as
cagey as she was smart. Her dark blue
trouser suit hugged her curvaceous
figure, hinting at a voluptuous bosom.
Back in the seventies, it was forbidden
for women to wear trouser suits. How he
wished he could have been the prime
minister then. 'No, not COVID.
Something much worse.'

She appeared surprised. 'What
could possibly be worse than COVID?
Don't tell me the American president is
coming over for another visit. It really

isn't a good time, Rupert. The Welsh are not fans.'

'No, not him', Streaker assured her. 'It's come to my attention that you have been discussing forming an alliance of independent states with Scotland and Northern Ireland, divorcing the UK.'

'You do have good sources, Rupert. I've always admired you for that.' Her smile retained a friendliness that appeared genuine.

'So, you don't deny it?'

'Why should I when we're simply talking hypothetically?'

'Are you telling me there's no real substance to the rumour?' he persisted, watching for any sign that she would prefer to discuss another topic.

'I'm saying that we're playing with the notion, weighing the pros and cons.

It's not even a hypothetical decision that we'd take lightly. You appreciate that Wales as a country needs to review its position in the UK every now and again, just to be sure that we're receiving a fair portion of what Westminster hands out.' A note of harshness in her tone made him shift uneasily. It was true that Wales was not always the first at the trough when funds were distributed. The Welsh were indeed not always prominent in the mind of the government.

'If I wanted this hypothesis to go away, what would it cost me?' he asked Donna, holding her gaze.

'I'm not sure. What can you offer?'

'You're answering a question with a question, Donna.'

'I am, aren't I?' She dismissed the accusation as swiftly as it had been made, waiting for his response.

'I suppose I could suggest that a new company be set up in Wales. One that would bring direct and indirect jobs via suppliers and transport support. Could be worth millions to your economy.'

'Nice, but what else?'

'You want more?' he asked, astonished and a trifle irritated. Donna Davies always saw herself as his equal, as did her counterparts in Scotland and Northern Ireland. Her demands reflected that and more. What confronted him was not a hypothesis. The three of them had gone much further than that, much further than even Bandip's sources had apprised them of. 'What else?'

'Additional hundred million each for education, health, and infrastructure.'

'That's three hundred million at a time when we're stretched due to COVID.'

'Ask some of your chums to pay their taxes instead of squirreling it away in some offshore shell company.'

'I'll see what I can do. Is that everything?'

'I want the government to move out of London.'

He hadn't seen it coming but was aware of the argument that the government needed to be physically centralised. 'I suppose you want us to move to Cardiff or Swansea?'

'No, Rupert. I want government moved further North. I'd like for it to be in Blackburn.'

'That would cost a fortune.'

'You can stagger it. Moving departments at six-month intervals. The parliament can be the last to move. We could have a new building constructed that can actually accommodate us all at the same time instead of ministers having to stand around, waiting for seats to be made available. A physically central relocation will also demonstrate that the government intends to treat everyone the same. That elusive level playing field can finally be a dream come true. You could make it happen, Rupert. You'd go down in history as not only a man of the people but someone that's loved by the people.'

Streaker fell silent. Loved by the people. History reflecting that he stood head and shoulders above his predecessors, bringing all four nations closer than they had ever been by relocating to a central region of the UK. It was all he had ever wanted – the love of the British public. 'You do appreciate how much of a challenge such an undertaking would be for me? What assurances do I have that you will keep your word once I get you all that you ask?'

'First, I need to see credible moves on your part towards the goals I've set as well as some tangible progress before I offer any assurances. Hypothetically, I imagine even if you start today, it will take at least twelve months before you're able to produce anything that appears remotely like the scenario I've set for you.'

'And what assurances can I expect at the end of those twelve months?'

'During and at the end of the twelve months, you will receive my full support. However, in the event that you do not meet my expectations, I will likely fall back on the hypothesis reached with Scotland and Northern Ireland.' She paused. 'I'd like the money as soon as possible. I'm sure you'll be able to persuade your chums that it's in their interests to help out.'

'You have my word that I'll do all I can to secure this hypothetical arrangement', he told her, still thinking about the love of the British people and the potential size of the statue that would be built in his honour. At least a foot taller than any other. It would likely be constructed in Blackburn, outside the new parliament building. He could see it clearly. More clearly than he had been able to visualise anything else that his time as prime minister would be remembered for.

She left him alone with his thoughts, the seed sown.

***

He didn't even notice Bandip join him until the other man coughed to attract his attention. Streaker returned to reality. 'Well, that wasn't easy. Cancel the war with Huvva. We've more important things to deal with.'

'Like?'

'Some progress has been made. She was at least willing to negotiate.' He then went on to explain her demands and waited while Bandip absorbed their negotiations.

'I knew I shouldn't have left you two alone. She's a wily woman who knows just how to play you.'

'Play me!' Streaker sat up as if from the shock of being scalded by a hot iron. 'She didn't play me.'

Bandip knew Streaker too well, probably better than Streaker knew himself. His desire to mimic his personal political heroes had always been his Achilles' heel. Anyone who spent time with him would understand that soon enough. Davies would not have had to spend any more time with him than she had already. She had no doubt been waiting for the opportunity to sink her claws in. The opportunity had presented itself on a golden platter, and she had grabbed it with both hands. 'You can't do it, Rupert.'

'What can't I do?'

'Move the government to Blackburn. For heaven's sake! Do you understand how much it would cost?' On the one hand, he was arguing with Streaker about costs while his capacity to multi-task had another part of his mind considering the potential construction companies owned by chums of theirs. 'We'd have to raise taxes, and the public won't appreciate that. They're broke as it is, and who knows how badly off they'll be after we've finally finished with the COVID restrictions. We have to grow the economy, not create more obstacles for it.' He finished with the name of a worthy construction company in mind: Build-Quick-Build-For-Today. Sir Harold Dash, its owner, was known for undercutting all his competitors. Quality was not a strong suit of theirs; however, frequent maintenance to keep buildings standing for years attracted consistent income for years to follow. 'You seriously need to think long and hard about this, Rupert.'

'I agree that the costs will be significant, but the return on investment will also prove worthwhile. Job creation will go through the roof. All this with essential improvements in infrastructure between London and Blackburn, and therefore the north. The Northern Powerhouse will become a reality rather than an overused dodge to maintain support. I can see the whole idea doing plenty of good all round.'

'People won't like the idea of moving the government to Blackburn,

Rupert. Their roots are in London, alongside the Queen. And what will Her Majesty have to say about it? There isn't a castle or a palace for her there. Where's she going to stay when she needs to visit? You can hardly put her up at a local B and B!'

'What about Lancaster Castle? It's been there since the 11th century and has been undergoing a huge refurbishment. What better place for the Queen to be located than in one of the country's oldest castles? I'm sure she'll agree. She at least still puts the country first.'

'As do we all, Rupert, but what about the need to be in the heart of the capital for the parliament to properly understand the needs of the people? Ministers can travel here more easily than they can to the north.'

'Well, that's part of the problem, Jonathon. We'd be taking on a huge necessary change to bring all the people closer, to actually understand their needs.'

'And what about the needs of the ministers, Rupert? Don't they count? I mean the Lords is full of old pensioners who can just about make it to the front door without falling asleep from exhaustion. You'll be cutting them off from working for the country, not to mention depriving them of a source of income. It seems very unfair.'

'The Lords needs rejigging. We both know that. The public is tired of the aged representatives receiving three hundred a day for just showing up and either hanging around for five minutes after collecting their cash or having a nap on the benches. Television cameras should never have been allowed into such a place. A move away from

London will prove beneficial both to the government and the safekeeping of the Union. We can always turn the old parliament buildings into historical places of interest and charge tourists a fortune to see them. The more I think about it, the more I'm convinced that it's the right thing to do. Ministers will have to accept that times have changed. They need to look at the broader picture. Splitting the Union is a non-starter, whatever the cost. Relocating to Blackburn shows the Scots that we're willing to commit to changes that will help us all better understand their issues. It will be the same for all northerners, including the Irish.'

'What about the people who matter?'

'Everyone matters, Jonathon.' He smiled.

'But some matter more than the others, Rupert, and to believe otherwise is both naïve and foolish. You can't afford to make enemies out of your colleagues simply to placate what is possibly Donna Davies' ploy to do just that.'

'I've no doubt that you're right to a point. She is wily, and creating a rift among our numbers would be one of her aims. But that doesn't deter from the fact that there actually is sufficient credibility in her plan to move us out of London and still achieve our agenda by doing so, perhaps more easily even.'

'At least meet with the cabinet and get their opinions before committing to this. If they're totally against it, it will give you some idea of how the rest of the party might feel.'

'I know at least three who will like the idea of moving north. Making life easier for them will override all else.' Momentarily studying Bandip, he sucked in a deep breath. 'What else is bothering you?'

'I'm not fully convinced that the Scots, the Welsh, and the Northern Irish are ready to jump ship. If they took a referendum and won, it would require at least two years of effort on their part for the divorce to become effective. Time is on our side.'

'There's a new election in May 2024. It isn't as far away as it sounds. We need to begin the process of winning that election now. I want the result of the next election to be a foregone conclusion. A landslide for us even! Because the public sees that we're doing all the right things, for all the right reasons. We can achieve that and our inherited agenda by moving the government to Blackburn. I believe it could even lose the SNP seats. It may even give us a chance to win back some of them and keep Labour out. It's an opportunity I can't ignore.'

'Relocating the government isn't going to sway the voters as much as you're hoping it will.'

'You can't be sure, and neither can I. What we can be certain of is the fact that it will create jobs and wealth between London and Blackburn. And also improve rail and road infrastructures. Who knows what else! I want time to think it over, because right this minute I'm beginning to believe that she was right and you're wrong. But what I promise to do is pass it by the cabinet before making any announcements.'

Bandip reluctantly conceded. Thinking about moving from his home in Belgravia to Blackburn was extremely unattractive.

CHAPTER FOUR

The power of public funding

For twenty minutes, Kate Allfores sat in her car in the underground carpark, before the passenger door opened and Rupert Streaker joined her. His bodyguard remained outside, positioned by the door. 'This is very inconvenient, Kate. Not to say, dangerous. Jessica has as many spies as my rivals.'

'I'm sure it's not as inconvenient as being stuck in a nuclear fallout shelter without any heating, Rupert!'

'If Jessica found out about this meeting, even a nuclear fallout shelter wouldn't save us.'

'You promoted Bernard and demoted me. You think that's fair?'

'Not at all, Kate', he replied in a calm, soothing tone. 'Your move was a lateral transfer. Blame it on that blasted tattoo of Lassie, not me.'

'You used to say you liked it', she reminded him.

He could remember it all too well and felt a stir deep within him. Quickly brushing such thoughts aside, he asked, 'Why am I here?'

'I can't do this anymore, Rupert. It's not fair.'

'It's only been a fortnight, Kate. You need to give me more time before I can arrange another move without drawing attention.'

'How long?'

'Six months.'

'Six months! You must be joking. When Jonathon persuaded me to move, he left out the part about it being a term of imprisonment. I don't deserve this over a shag. Especially because you instigated it and seemed to enjoy it as much as I did.'

'Of course, you don't, and of course I did.'

'It was nice to catch up on old times.' She moved a little closer to him, just enough for her perfume to tingle his senses. 'Surely there's something you can do to help relieve my situation. I'm so unhappy at home. He hasn't been near me since the headline hit the stands. I've never felt so unwanted. Even you don't want me anymore. I feel like I've just been cast off.'

'That's not true. You know you're often in my thoughts, but Bernard was extremely forceful. He had us over a barrel, especially because you told him about our latest tryst. Why did you do that?'

'He hit me. I couldn't take it.'

'But you didn't have any bruises', he said.

'Not any place it would show,' she told him with a sigh. 'Let's not talk about it.'

'Has he hit you before?' Streaker asked with artificial concern. Knowing that her husband could be violent was, however, important, as it might mean that he was in physical danger.

'Only when he thinks I've done something wrong. Otherwise, he's quite gentle.'

'And you've still stayed with him all this time?'

'My work has kept me occupied. That's why it's so important to me. It makes me feel wanted, gives me something to focus on besides my marriage. Please help me, Rupert. Move me as soon as you can. I'll be eternally grateful,' she finished with watery eyes that made his resistance crumble into insignificance. She moved closer, their mouths meeting. The bodyguard faced away from the car as they intertwined on the front seat.

***

Bandip had been busy phoning construction contacts all day, setting the groundwork for potential companies that were likely to prove useful creating the new parliament buildings as well as the transport infrastructure around them. there was no time to waste if he wanted to keep Streaker happy. He needed to show willingness before the Cabinet meeting. Otherwise, his research might prove to be a complete waste of time. However, the process definitely had opened his eyes to the potential of creating a very lucrative income stream. No wonder ministers were eager to discuss such things with contacts they felt comfortable and secure. Agreements spread over a five-year period meant regular payments to an offshore account. It made him rethink his objections, made him consider that perhaps Streaker was right to agree to Davies' proposals. After all, did any of it really matter in the end? people would have new parliament buildings in the north would be more accessible to the people than the current ancient and totally inadequate buildings in London. Besides, in five years, he'd be living someplace like the Seychelles, far away from London and politics.

As Streaker returned to his office, Bandip joined him, carrying papers that sketched out provisional costs for a main building with temporary accommodation for all six-hundred-and-fifty ministers. Three bedroomed luxury apartments were designed to provide accommodation for family members, if required. After his favourite contractor had provided a starting figure in the billions, he was convinced of the need for the parliament to move. 'I thought you'd want to see some draft costs for a new parliament building as well as the accommodation for all the ministers. It's a starting point that will bear little resemblance to the end cost, but it's necessary when you present the scheme to the cabinet.'

Streaker's eyes widened as he took in the total cost. 'We need someone we can trust to be in charge.'

'Surely that will be up to the minister for housing and planning?'

'Not bloody likely! This has to have my name all over it. We can't afford mistakes. I've already got someone in mind. He's very methodical, practical, and honest.'

Bandip was already disappointed. 'They're clearly not a member of the cabinet. Whom do you have in mind?'

'Bernard Allfores.'

'What!'

'Check his record. I have. He'll do brilliantly. He's painstaking over everything, and he'll need to be. This scenario will be so full of snipers that we'll need someone who can fend off all comers. Allfores can do that.' He momentarily paused. 'Except for one possibly indirect issue. Kate told me that he sometimes hits her when he thinks she did something wrong, like our little encounter.'

'I don't think that would be unexpected', Bandip said.

'Perhaps, but it's the type of thing that could wind up generating adverse public opinion. We need to make sure that this type of thing doesn't get out.'

'Supposedly only Kate knows about it, and if she hasn't shared that with anyone else, then it remains a secret.'

'Check with her when you tell her about the new positing she's been assigned. I'll talk to him about it the next time we meet. For now, we play it as though there're are no hidden skeletons in his cupboard.'

'What about Monica Moon? She comes across as someone with the intellect to do well and doesn't appear to have any hidden secrets in her cupboard.'

'No Jonathon, my mind's made up. it came to me a couple of hours ago. This will him close, where all my enemies need to be. No wriggle room. The icing on the cake is that he'll do a damn good job. Giving the opportunity to a pleb, someone with no real heritage or status in our own ranks, the public will see this promotion as a genuine move towards equality. They'll love it.'

'But he's a statistician. He's never worked in construction.'

'That's never stopped us before. Most of the cabinet have never worked in the areas they administer.'

'I know, Rupert, but that's why we have so many cock-ups. Remember that thing with the ferries? It wasted millions, and the public knows it. If Allfores drops a clanger like that, we could be in serious trouble.'

'If he does, and I don't for believe he will a moment, then we can point at his background and claim that we tried giving someone without our background a chance, but he sadly failed. The public will have to acknowledge it and believe that we really are better than them.' He was grinning so widely that he could hardly continue speaking. 'Giving him the job also stops any backlash from the statistics office over his accelerated promotion. This couldn't have worked out better had I planned it myself.'

'And what title are you considering giving him in this role?' Bandip asked dubiously.

'Minister for parliament relocation.'

'What about the parliament buildings in London? He can't be expected to deal with them as well as the new buildings and infrastructure.'

'No, of course not', Streaker said. 'I think Kate Allfores can be put in charge of managing the old estate.'

'You're joking! Please tell me you're being funny.'

'She earned the respect of her colleagues as an under-secretary. She's good at this kind of thing. We both know it. So, we need to take advantage of her skillset.'

'You're forgetting that any credibility she may have won was lost immediately her backside with Lassie tattooed on was exposed to the public!'

'She deserves better than we gave her', Streaker said.

'What's Bernard Allfores going to think?'

'That I'm attempting to repair their marriage by putting them in close proximity in the workplace. There's no way I'd be doing that if I were still diddling her. Goes without saying, doesn't it? Jessica will be satisfied.'

Bandip's unhappy expression made him curious. 'Okay, there's something more than my shagging that's bothering you. What is it?'

'His honesty. You saw how much the new building and accommodation will cost. That kind of money cannot be handed to someone as honest as Allfores.'

'He's hardly likely to steal any of it', Streaker said.

'Precisely my point!'

He shrugged. 'So, you'll need to be more innovative than usual. You enjoy a challenge. I'm sure you'll work around it. Don't forget all the contractors will be friendlies. They'll help you work something out. Allfores will simply be our camouflage for the mere chance that anything goes wrong – the one to take all the flak.'

'Maybe', he replied.

'Plus, with his wife managing the old estate, it'll seem like they're both involved.'

'You'd sell her out?'

'There are some things that are more important than a good shag.' He smiled. 'Not many, I grant you, but personal survival is one of them. You're my top fixer. Negative words are not common in your vocabulary. I hope you're not suggesting that this pleb might present an insurmountable problem for you?'

Bandip knew he was being played. He was well aware of the tactics Streaker employed when he wanted things to go his way between them. 'Of course not, Rupert.'

'Good. Because there's more. Kate has some ideas about changes to the House of Lords.'

'Kate!' His breath got caught in his chest. 'So, you've already been in contact with her?'

'She called me. She's having a dreadful time with the nuclear fall-out shelter project. There's no heating in most of them, so they're bloody freezing. She doesn't deserve that.'

'You've seen her, haven't you?' Bandip's eyes narrowed.

'We met in an underground carpark. Only my driver Pete was present, and he's a hundred percent loyal. No one will know.'

'Tell me you didn't shag her again.'

'I didn't shag her again', he replied flatly.

'You're lying. For heaven's sake, Rupert! How can I protect you if you're going to keep repeating the same mistake!'

'It probably won't happen again. I've taken care of things as I've already explained to you.'

'You can't afford to let it happen again. I mean it. If the media ever gets a sniff of anything going on between the two of you, I won't be able to save you from them, or Jessica.' He shook his head as if to clear it. 'So, tell me. What little surprises does Kate have for the Lords?'

'Well, she rightly suggests that the public view most of the Lords as parasites, collecting three hundred each time they visit. Fifteen hundred quid a week for falling asleep seems a bit much, even to me. She has some pretty radical ideas that will do away with the old system of heritage, although that's already on its way out. However, her idea is to retain the House of Lords, but as a third measure to counter government policy rather than a second. She wants us to introduce a completely new level called the Public Gallery. Representatives will be from both business and public services, nominated by their own employees. The Public Gallery will act in a similar fashion as the American congress. The House of Lords will retain the power to contest government legislation but only as be limited to human rights and environmental issues. The attendance fee will be dropped. People who wish to serve in the Lords will do so for free other; of course, the expenses incurred with to travel stationery and so on will be reimbursed.'

'They won't like that', Bandip declared, already imagining the Lords in uproar. 'You can't take away their attendance fee. It's a part of their income.'

'They'll hardly starve, Jonathon. That fifteen hundred pounds a week could be better spent elsewhere. There are eight hundred of the blighters. That's more than a million quid per annum! If we said we'd use that to help finance the new Public Gallery, the public will think it a great idea. They positively hate the Lords for siphoning off so much, having seen so many asleep on the benches. We have to be realistic. The Lords is well overdue a shake-up.'

'You might think it's money for old rope, but a few of them actually do some good', Bandip insisted. Too many friends and relatives enjoyed the Lords for a get-together to discuss the future and their next holiday destination. His family would be upset if anything changed, especially anything financial.

'You're in danger of upsetting so many who matter if you go ahead with this that I don't know how I'll be able to protect you from your own colleagues. Let me warn you, Rupert. You're playing with fire just because you enjoy shagging an old school crush.'

'Well, first, she not an old school crush. Although I had always fancied her. Second, we're on the verge of losing public support as well as quite a few colleagues if we continue on the road we've already taken. We need to do something that offers at least one of those groups hope, and I believe if we can gain public support eventually our colleagues will have to join us.' He sucked in a deep breath and continued, 'Kate will see to it that the current parliament buildings serve as historical monuments. Tourists will love them. We can charge the earth and recover what the costly refurbishment has cost. After that, we'll be in profit. Everyone will gain from this, Jonathon, I promise. Stick with me, and I'll guarantee that you won't lose out.'

'The risks are great', said Bandip, his tone neutral.

'We take risks every day. This one is no different other than offering the biggest payday at the end of it. Come on, let's have a drink', Streaker said, pulling a desk drawer open and taking out two glasses and a bottle of Glavar whiskey.

***

'Is nothing sacred?' Streaker said, his eyes fixed on a security photograph taken at the underground carpark where he and Kate Allfores had secretly met.

'We couldn't get your driver to rat on you if that's any consolation, Rupert.'

'It isn't', he replied glumly. 'You can't go anywhere these days without being recorded on CCTV. Bloody nuisance!'

'The security guard is a relative of one of my minister's. You don't have to worry. Neither of them will speak a word about this indiscretion. We've all been there. I think it's rather a good shot of your backside with Kate's face peering over your shoulder in ecstasy. Also, how did she manage to get her legs so high? Must be extremely flexible for her age! She really is something, isn't she?'

'Alright Rex, you've got me dead to rights. What does Labour want in order to keep the lid sealed on my private life?'

Rex Pounding was visiting the prime minister in his office, loaded with an intention to blackmail. Prior to offering an answer, he surveyed the room with the eye of someone looking forward to becoming its new owner. Sadly, he thought the big picture did not include putting Streaker through matrimonial dilemma even if he did deserve it. 'Rumour has it that you're intending to present a monumental project to the parliament.'

'How much do you know?' he asked, returning the photograph. The underground surveillance video was something he and Kate Allfores hadn't considered.

'Just that it's about relocating the parliament. I can fill in some of the empty spaces for myself, but I want to know the general plan before you present it to the cabinet.'

There was no point holding back. Streaker needed to have him on side, just to preserve his marriage and keep public peace. When he was done explaining, the two men sat staring at each other without a word passing between them for a full minute.

'We were thinking of nominating someone from our benches to take on the role of program director. Eddie Edifice's name sprang to mind. Is that a problem?'

'I've already assigned the post. It could not be someone from our circle. That was paramount for retaining public support. Bernard Allfores will be leading the entire programme.'

'Allfores! You mean Kate's husband?'

'I do.'

Pounding fell silent again. Another minute passed. 'I see where you're coming from, Rupert, but I insist that you allow one of my people to take the lead.'

It was Streaker's turn to fall silent. When he finally spoke, he said, 'How about a compromise? Let Allfores take the initial lead. If he stumbles, we can blame it on inexperience and your bloke automatically takes over. While Allfores is running things, Edifice can shadow him. That way, you get as much publicity as us, and in the event that things go tits up, you're seen as the saviour. It's a win for the both of us. Co-operation is the key to keeping the public on our side.'

'Not a bad idea. Nice to know that you have one now and then that doesn't include shagging the arse off Allfores' wife.'

'That was uncalled for, Rex.'

'It's a reminder why we're both here, having this conversation. Just in case it slips your mind', Pounding said with a steely gaze. 'Very well then. We'll go with your plan. Now what about the old parliament buildings? I'm sure you have a coordinator in mind.'

'Kate Allfores,' he said quickly.

'Bloody hell!' Pounding leaned forward on the seat. 'You do like playing with fire, Rupert. Are you serious?'

'She's good. Look at her track record. She's ideal for the job. Besides, this way, no one will suspect that we'd been at it. Not with her husband working so close.'

'I learned a long time ago to remain loyal to my wife. Women have a habit of finding out when their partners have dallied elsewhere. Jessica may appear like butter wouldn't melt in her mouth, but I'm sure just like every other woman she has a streak of vindictive punishment for a partner who betrays her trust.'

'No doubt. But do you have a problem with Kate Allfores?'

'I was going to suggest Fiona Brickie. However, we can operate on the same terms as we are with her husband.'

'Agreed.' Streaker was satisfied. Nothing more likely to upset the precarious set-up with either Allfore.

'It seems like we've almost successfully overcome the first hurdle, Rupert,' Pounding said without any indication that he was satisfied. 'However, the best is yet to come. We'd like to allow the public an opportunity to invest in all aspects of this programme. Each program project will attract specific outcomes. For example, we believe a toll road circling the new parliament estate would be appropriate. The security aspects of having a circular by-pass around the estate are obvious, as is the necessity to maintain traffic flow. Allowing the public to make affordable investments will be seen as caring by the public. We will support it, and I believe the other parties will as well. It will also offset the fresh taxes needed. Plus, it may also be seen as a promise to build genuinely good council housing outside the parliament estate for workers at the estate to live. All at a rate that would make renting them affordable.'

'Mmmh. Very well. What else?'

'We want two critical services nationalised. The NHS and the railways.'

'Not a chance', Streaker scoffed. 'Private investment in both is just too useful.'

'Not my problem.' Pounding eyed him without sympathy. 'Your amorous blunder comes at a high cost, Rupert.

We want you to set the scenario in which you put forward plans to nationalise both. By doing so, you'll gain public support as well as our back. That I can assure you.'

'But its fundamentally against everything my party stands for, against all that's been happening over the past fifty years. I can't just tear everything up and say that we're returning to the good old days of nationalisation. My minister would throw a fit!'

'You're a devious political mediator, Rupert. I have every faith in your ability to sway your party away from its fanatical intention to privatise everything for personal gain. Convince them that you think it's time they put the country ahead of their own financial interests.'

'They'll dump me', Streaker replied. A vision of his colleagues demanding his resignation was already vivid in his mind's eye. 'I can't possibly do that. If I'm gone, what use can I be of to you? You at least have a chance of manipulating things your way with me here.'

Pounding had guessed his reaction, knew also that what he way saying was true. Having a malleable prime minister was far better than having a hostile one. 'We didn't expect you to do this overnight. What we want is to see you making the right moves to create a scenario in which nationalisation becomes the only option.'

'And how do you propose I do that?'

'Privatisation has to fail. It's the only way. The public will openly demand a return to nationalisation then. We've seen it time and again with the railways.

With regard to the health service, do the opposite of what you've already done to the NHS, making it appear second rate compared to private medical care. Turn the tables. Hand out generous pay rises to medical staff so they can afford to remain. Increase the number of hospitals around the country. Cut waiting times to minutes rather than months. Basically, Rupert, stop what you're doing to harm the NHS and start bringing it back from the precipice you've taken it to over the past ten years. The public will love you for it.'

'My party will destroy me for it', he glumly muttered.

'Not with the public, us, and the other parties behind you. Even your chums couldn't fight us all.'

Streaker sighed. Rarely had he felt so beaten. So, defeated. 'Is there anything else?'

Pounding, in contrast, appeared happy and pleased with himself. 'Of course, but then you would have been disappointed if I hadn't gone for as much as possible. Education is next on the agenda. We want the suspension of charitable support towards private schools in order to see to the fact that they are more equal to schools under the public education authority. Additionally, the unions require a new law stating that each company with more than a hundred employees must have a union representative present on their management board.'

'It'll be seen as a Communist take-over.'

'It will be seen as employees getting a fair voice at management board meetings,' Pounding corrected. 'Socialism isn't the scary beast you suggest it is. Doing more for the public is actually a good thing, Rupert, whatever you and your chums may think.'

'If you want that, I'd be remiss agreeing to it without requiring restrictions to the actions taken by union representatives who are given access to management's confidential negotiations with ordinary employees. Also, it would be unseemly for union representatives to incite employees to down tools, abusing their position and the information they might've gained from it. Management must be given time to express to its employees how it sees a company's future and also any changes in terms and conditions of employment before the union representatives speak out. Only after management has expressed itself can a union representative discuss with employees their opinion and what they consider the appropriate course of action to be. For me, to do otherwise would be a blatant disregard for the necessity of management's confidential information to protect a company not only from revealing unsavoury changes to its employees but also allow rivals to be better positioned in the marketplace.'

'I want time to discuss your suggestion with my people.'

'How long do you need?'

'A week. There's no rush, is there?'

He recalled Kate Allfores' plea to get her out of the nuclear fallout shelters sooner rather than later. Any delay could not be helped. Besides, plans had to be put in motion to get Bernard Allfores ready to lead the new parliament programme. Telling him would be the starting point. Although, he didn't doubt that Bernard would be overjoyed to take on such a responsibility. Right up until he discovered that his wife would be leading the management of the old parliament buildings. Streaker had not yet formalised the words to introduce it into their conversation. Avoiding any possible suggestion that he had spoken with Kate since the scandalous headline had broken would prove difficult. 'I'm sure a week won't damage plans.'

To say that Streaker appeared morose after Pounding had left would be an understatement. Bandip sensed trouble, and although unsighted, he felt that Allfores was somehow involved.

'What did he want?'

'Close the door, and come sit with me', Streaker said, reaching for the bottle of Glavar and two glasses. 'I think I might've bitten off more than I can chew this time.'

Bandip sat down. He allowed Streaker some time to get his thoughts in some order before talking, passing a half-filled glass towards him across the desk.

'Kate and I were caught on a security camera in the underground carpark we met. He got his hands on a copy. There's no wriggle room. If it gets out, I'm done for in more ways than one. Pounding wants to manipulate me to do his party's bidding. It's a total disaster. I may have to resign. Quit politics altogether.'

'Steady on, Rupert. That's a trifle drastic. There's no such thing as no wriggle room. All we need do is find a way out of this.' Bandip hoped he sounded reassuring. The loss of Rupert Streaker was not something he wanted to consider. It was not something that would help him. 'I take it Pounding is keeping this matter a closely guarded secret.'

'It would be useless to him if he didn't. He's better off with me working as prime minister to get what he wants.'

'And his evidence is this security video.'

'I know what you're thinking, but he'll have dozens of copies by now. There's no way stealing the one he has in his office or at home will be enough.'

'That's not what I'm thinking', Bandip said. 'We have to draw him out, show him that blackmailing you would be as bad for him as the security video is for you. No one in public office can afford to be caught out as a blackmailer.'

'What do you have in mind?' Streaker asked, suddenly interested. The gloom seemed to be lifting.

'When do you intend to meet again?'

'He needs a week. He wants seven days to speak to his colleagues about our arrangement.'

'Gosh, you mean he's going to share the blackmail stuff with his colleagues. I say, that's bloody fabulous!'

'It is?'

'Of course, it is. You'll need to get him to say it on video. It means that we get not only him but all the others who agree to the blackmail as well. I think this could work out very well indeed.' Bandip looked and sounded cheerful. The fixer was about to prove that he was worth every penny.

CHAPTER FIVE

The possibility of a problem

Prime Minister's Questions Time was thinly attended by ministers on both sides of the House. The social distancing due to COVID were maintained against any arguments offered by Number 10 to ignore the law, much to Streaker's acute disappointment. His latest appearance made no change to his desire for advisers to be close at hand instead of out of earshot. Confronted by Rex Pounding once again, he was reminded of just how useful they had proven in the past. Yet, there was a difference. Pounding had not attacked him. Not once. As if signalling just how easy he could make both their lives.

'I ask the prime minister when we'll have an opportunity to view his draft project related to the building of a bridge between Scotland and Northern Ireland. I fully appreciate that his attention has needed to be focused on COVID these past months, but this is an issue that he raised when he was elected. Just how far has it progressed, if at all?'

Streaker rose from his seat. 'I can confirm that the project remains under consideration. It should be appreciated that we have sourced tenders from several construction firms. After we have some idea about the costs, we'll need to decide whether they justify its construction. Additionally, we'll be reviewing whether we might offer the public shares in the bridge, which will be a toll bridge to recover the cost. For example, the Dartford toll tunnel built in the 60s has more than paid for itself. We envisage that shares in the bridge will prove to be a good long-term investment.'

'Thank you, Prime Minister.' Pounding remained seated while others stood up with further questions. There was nothing controversial from the other side of the House, part of the arrangement with Pounding.

After Question Time was over, Streaker and Pounding met outside briefly. Streaker smiled in an unusually friendly manner. 'Have you had a chance to discuss our issues?'

'Yes', he replied. 'I think we should probably agree our intention to move forward and leave it to our teams to tweak out any glitches.'

'Good. What about later today, say 5, at my office?' Streaker asked without wishing to appear too eager.

'See you there, Rupert', Pounding strode away without saying more. He was so confident that he had the upper hand that it was impossible for him to imagine that anything could go wrong.

As soon as he was out of sight, Sir Roger Rabid, the Tory chief whip, joined Streaker, red-faced and grim. 'What was that?'

'What was what, Roger?'

'Offering shares to the public, that's what. Since when do we behave like that?'

'Times are changing, Roger. We need to be a little more benevolent towards the public if we want to remain in the driver's seat. I'm starting to prepare for the next election early.'

'Four years early seems a trifle unnecessary, Rupert. If you're good to them this soon, they'll be expecting bigger offers in exchange for their votes in 2024. You know what they're like. Human nature makes them that way. Never satisfied with what we're giving them. Always looking for that little bit extra. Only in 24, it'll be much more than just a little bit extra if you hand things out now!'

'They've taken a hammering, Roger. COVID, Brexit, immigration – the list goes on. We need to give them hope that things will improve. Also, that its only our government that can give them what they're seeking. We need to make Labour appear as if its past its sell-by-date. The type of people it used to represent no longer exists, except in small clutches. A few miners. Stevedores, longshoremen, dockers. Nothing like the number we had back in the 1960s. That's when they had real power. Today, we have a huge workforce in finance. And they are not the type to vote Labour.'

'What about nurses, paramedics, and so on?'

'And how well are they doing?' He chuckled.

'Yes, your strategy is working. However, not giving them a pay rise as a way to force them to quit the NHS isn't sustainable.'

'The figures show growth in the number of agency staff available.'

'If you let me finish, Rupert,' Rabid said flatly. 'It's unsustainable when politicians are seen to be giving themselves a healthy pay rise. The public are going to figure it, out and there will be a backlash when they do.'

'We need to make a statement to the NHS staff, Roger. They can't believe they're in the driver's seat. Our pay rise demonstrates that we can get away with whatever we need. Besides, by the time the public have twigged, it'll be too late. The NHS will be history.' He scoffed. 'I'm taking the initiative in a big way, Roger. We need to modernise our thinking. Change is necessary for everyone. Including us.'

'Poppycock! You're attacking the livelihoods of our colleagues' friends and families. If there's a bridge, they're the ones who should be collecting from it and not the bloody public!' Rabid was an ardent champion for the Tory cause of generating wealth for a select few – the reason he had been chosen as its chief whip. Now in his mid-fifties, he had survived countless attempts to rout him from the position by younger opponents. Demonstrating that he could beat them all amused him. He was too well-placed and established for anyone to simply step into his shoes. Most importantly, he was a survivor with a nose that warned him when things were askew. Right now, his nose was on fire. 'I'm not sure what game you're playing, Rupert, but be warned that you've come very close to the edge of a deep dark precipice from which there will be no turning back if it happens again. I'm shocked that you failed to keep me up-to-speed with this strategy.'

Being threatened by your own chief whip was not unusual when the party agenda was seen as vulnerable. 'What I do is always for the good of the party, Roger. I don't always share my strategies because there are too many leaks, but you can rest assured that I have a plan that will make us appear as the equality party of this country only by arranging a few investment tweaks. I'll explain them to you once I'm ready.'

Standing up to Rabid was always the best course of action. He understood strength, and although he was upset at not being included in a new strategy, he would accept it for a limited time. 'There's something else I wanted to discuss with you', he said, swiftly moving on. 'Horace Horny has done it again, and I was hoping you might consider having the girl visit you to calm things down. She might be amenable to your persuasive techniques with the ladies, Rupert. Apparently, she's a huge admirer.'

'How many does this make?'

'Five', Rabid replied unhappily. 'The next assistant he gets will be male, I promise. He only got another young woman because his father asked for her on his behalf.'

'And does Lord Horny realise what his son is putting us through?'

'He does and sends his apologies. He also intends on writing him out of one of the family estates he was giving him in his will as a gesture of good faith.'

'Who is this young woman? What's her name?'

'Jennifer Juggs. She's a twenty-five-year-old legal researcher. A very nice and friendly person by all accounts.'

'Who doesn't appreciate being groped', Streaker finished. 'Tell her to meet me at my office at 3 this afternoon. I can spare ten minutes. But this is positively the last time, Roger. I don't care how much of the UK his father owns!'

***

Jennifer Juggs arrived punctually and sat in front of the prime minister's large mahogany desk, wearing a wide-eyed expression that suggested Rabid that had been correct about her admiration for Streaker. 'I must apologise in advance for having to meet you under such gross circumstances, Miss Juggs.

It was raining outside, and she had removed her coat before entering the room, leaving it with a security guard. She was dressed in a thin, close-fitting jumper and a knee-length tartan skirt. Her dark hair was tied back in a bun, allowing her chubby but pretty features more visibility. She looked the part of a legal researcher. A book worm. However, Streaker did not fail to notice that her two most prominent features jutted defiantly out towards him like ice cream cones. In some twisted way, it made him sympathise with Horace Horny. 'Please call me Jennifer, Prime Minister.'

He smiled. 'Thank you, Jennifer. I know this must be an extremely difficult position for you to be in. I know it is for me.' She smiled. He was winning. 'Could you tell me what actually happened so I can better appreciate the circumstances.'

'Certainly, Prime Minister. I was standing by the coffee maker, reaching for a cup from the cabinet above it, when Mr Horny came up behind me and cupped my breasts.'

'Did he say anything?'

'Bloody hell, I think', she replied. 'Yes, bloody hell.'

'And what did you do?'

'I slapped his hands away and then slapped his face. I also told him I was going to report him.'

'Did he say anything else?'

'He apologised, but I was so angry that he thought so little of me to have the courage to just come up and touch me like that. I may have overreacted, I suppose. I mean I wasn't expecting anything like that from him. He's a married man.'

'Aren't we all', Streaker mumbled. 'Yes, of course. No, you didn't overreact. He was quite wrong to do such a thing. It's totally unacceptable for a man in his position to grope anyone without their consent. As your boss, he has a responsibility towards your health and safety. When did this happen?'

'This morning. At 10 a.m.'

'Have you discussed the matter with anyone else besides Mr Rabid?'

'No. I don't really want to get him into trouble. I just didn't want a repeat of what happened.'

'I can assure you nothing like this will ever happen again, Jennifer. You're in safe hands now, so to speak. Are you willing to leave the matter with me to deal with? I promise you he will suffer.'

'Thank you, Prime Minister. Yes. Knowing that you're dealing with it personally helps me a lot. Of course, I won't be able to return to work for him.'

'No worries. I'll make sure you get posted elsewhere. Is there a position you fancy yourself?'

She appeared surprised to be asked such a question. 'Well, I've always wanted to work for Stella Stump's legal team. Her knowledge on environmental law is second to none. I know I'd learn a lot to help my career.'

'I'll tell Stella to expect you. By the way, what grade are you currently?'

'I'm an EO, Prime Minister.'

'Well, from what Mr Rabid tells me after reading your report, you're deserving of a promotion. We'll bring it forward a few months so that you join Stella as an HEO.'

Jennifer Juggs was delighted. The sun truly shone from the darkest spot-on Rupert Streaker's body.

***

'Horace, it's Rupert Streaker', Streaker spoke into the phone in his office. 'I wanted you to know that I've sorted out another problem you created. Jennifer Juggs is leaving it to me to decide on an appropriate punishment. Also, she won't be returning to work for you.'

'I'm ever so grateful, Prime Minister.' Horny replied in a snivelling tone. 'I don't know what came over me.'

'You're an idiot, Horace. An idiot that your father and I have been forced to hide from the public for his family's sake. But that was positively the last time. If you can't keep your hands to yourself in the future, I'll be sure to kick you out of the party once and for all. Your too much of a liability.'

'I promise it won't ever happen again, Prime Minister.

'You said that the last four times, yet here we are with another molested young woman. Anyone else would've been locked up long ago.'

'I understand, Prime Minister.'

'Just make sure you do think about this. You and your father now owe me a debt. When I come calling for payment, it better not go ignored.'

'It won't', he replied.

'It better not be.' Streaker cradled the receiver with a sigh. At least there was one influential supporter he had if the proverbial shit ever hit the fan. He needed many, many more. Rabid was already suspicious. The man had a sixth sense when it came to figuring out subterfuge.

***

At 5 that afternoon, Rex Pounding visited Number 10 to set in motion their plans for the future. Full of confident bravado, he studied Streaker with the look of a champion about to be crowned. Streaker, on the other hand, remained impassive, largely restrained. Of late, his days had been fairly chaotic, but he hoped for a bit of peace and quiet after this meeting was done.

'Well, what did you and your associates decide?' Streaker started as the other man sat opposite him.

'We're in agreement with the arrangement that we discussed the other evening.'

'This needs to be clear for both of us Rex. Neither of us can afford a mistake that upsets the other. So, to be clear, is it your intention to withhold the photographs of my indiscretion as long as I remain malleable to your suggestions?'

'Of course, that's what I'm saying', Pounding replied, a trifle irritated that Streaker felt the need to spell it out in such basic terms.

'Fine, but what if you and your party ask me to do something that compromises my position as the prime minister?'

'There's no chance we'd do any such thing. You'll be acting on behalf of our party, in the interests of this country. You will not be working for a foreign government, Rupert. For the first time in your life, you'll actually be doing some good for the ordinary public instead of your rich chums.'

'If we didn't actually do anything for the public Rex, we wouldn't be in the government and you wouldn't be the leader of the opposition,' Streaker said before continuing. 'What's the first undertaking you intend on forcing me to do for your Party?'

'I've told you before, Rupert. Don't look on our arrangement as blackmail. Think of it more as a biased negotiation. You don't have a leg to stand on, and I'm making the most of the opportunity you've handed me.'

'Blackmail is what it is Rex, no matter how delicately you'd prefer to hear it.'

'You did well today with that business about public shares in the bridge. I watched Roger Rabid's face as he almost went ballistic. Giving to the

public is definitely never on his mind.'
He smiled, but Streaker's expression
showed no amusement. 'We want you
to start small. Something to whet our
appetites. A personal invitation to Sinn
Fein to attend the parliament. They're
paid for doing so, and it's about time
they did their job and represented the
people they claim support them.'

'You think that's a small issue?'
he asked.

'Compared to what we have in
mind, yes. Offering them a personal
invitation to attend the parliament will be
seen as the British government offering
an olive leaf. I'm sure the Republic will
support you.'

'I'll think about it', he said,
hesitant.

'No, Rupert. You'll do what we tell
you to. You have no choice. We expect

an answer by next week. If not, try again.'

Streaker leaned forward, his elbows on his desk, jaw jutting forward. 'Who else is included in this little group that's blackmailing me?'

'Why do you need to know that?'

'Because I demand to know if you want me to do things for you. You may have compromising photographs but don't expect me to simply nod my head and get on with things without knowing the identities of the people holding me at ransom. Any one of them could break off from you and sink my career and family.'

Pounding took a moment to consider this. 'Very well. Jonas Jury, Penelope Pollock, Terence Tweet, and Marilyn Masterly. No one else knows. You have my word on this.'

'What about the security guard who handed you the photo in the first place?'

'Masterly's cousin. He saw the photos but doesn't know anything about what we're using them for. Besides, the recording was deleted soon after he passed it to us.'

'You do understand that it's difficult for me to trust anything you say. You're a blackmailer. People don't get much lower than that.'

'I'm sure you'd have done the same thing, Rupert.'

'Never. My integrity does not allow me to do such a thing. No, you and your cartel are out there on your own, Rex.' He smiled unexpectedly, 'I think we've got enough now, Jonathon.'

Bandip entered the office, closing the door behind him.

'What's going on?' Pounding shifted around on the seat to face the other man.

'We've recorded this meeting, Rex', Bandip told him. 'We have you on tape, attempting to blackmail the prime minister of this country. We also have the names of your associates. If the security recording of the prime minister ever gets leaked to the media, the same will happen to our video. What Rupert did was wrong, but what you and your associates attempted was criminal. I have a police officer waiting outside if you decide to proceed and make public the security recording. You and the others will be arrested and held in custody pending a full police investigation, which will likely take months. I imagine the Labour party will be forced to find replacements for you and them as well.'

'You bastards!' Pounding stood up, his face red and eyes angrier than either of them had ever seen. 'You won't get away with this.'

'You'd better hope we do. Otherwise, you'll be spending time in prison. What would your wife and family have to say about that? I imagine when you finally get out, you'll be too old to think of taking up a new career.'

Pounding was furious. He stormed over to the door and turned back. 'Be smug while you can. This isn't over. Not by half. I don't like to be made to look like a fool. My people will be disappointed, but I will get back at both of you on my own!' He slammed the door behind him.

The two men stared at each other without speaking, then burst into laughter. 'Fantastic job, Jonathon.

Seeing him like that was worth going through hell.'

Bandip sat down, exhausted. 'You never quite know how things are going to turn out, but that was marvellous.'

Streaker strolled across to the window and stared out. The rain had stopped, and a blue sky had begun to emerge from behind the clouds.

'I suppose we don't have to think about relocating parliament now.'

'That hasn't changed', Streaker said.

'But we've crushed any chance of Pounding exposing you.'

'It's a good idea. We don't have too many of those running around this place at the moment. Everything I said about gaining public support because of it remains true, as do the long-term economic advantages. No, we keep on track with that one, Jonathon. Contact Bernard Allfores for me. Tell him to visit tomorrow at 10 a.m.'

Bandip smiled the Seychelles back into his future. 'I'll do that now', he said, quickly moving to the door and leaving Streaker alone.

The prime minister stared at the sky; the image of his statue a couple feet taller than it had previously been in his mind's eye.

***

With the prime minister occupied with Allfores the following morning, Bandip visited the parliament building for his subsidised breakfast in the restaurant. It would be a change from the meal he was offered at Number 10 but of the same high quality. He sat alone, his head buried in a tabloid, meal finished, when he heard the harsh tone of Roger Rabid just a few tables away. Keeping the newspaper high enough to remain anonymous, he looked to confirm that he had been correct about the voice and was surprised to discover that Rabid had been joined by Rex Pounding. As far as he knew, they were sworn enemies. Intrigued, he remained seated, reading his newspaper until they had finished an hour later and left in opposite directions.

***

Bernard Allfores appeared uncertain as he sat across from Streaker. The prime minister was, after all, the most powerful individual in the country, capable of stitching up just about anyone who offended him.

'Thanks for coming Bernard.'

'I could hardly say no', he replied flatly.

'I'm certain that you're not about to say no to what I'm going to offer you. At least not unless your next stop is an insane asylum.' He smiled, but Allfores remained impassive. 'I'm about to make public our intention to move the parliament to Blackburn, and I need a good chap to head the project. Since your promotion, you've become eligible for this job. Under the scrutiny of the appropriate minister, of course.'

Allfores wasn't certain that he had heard correctly. So, he asked, 'Relocating the parliament. And you want me to head the project?'

'Er, yes. Will you accept the posting? Of course, it's a long-term project. Minimum of five years. What do you say?'

'I'm shocked, Rupert', he said.

'I appreciate that, Bernard, but will you accept the posting?'

'Yes.'

'Good. Liaise with Jonathon. He'll help you with all you need. He's got tons of experience with these things and will steer you in the right direction for everything, including whom to use. Whatever your needs, listen to his advice.' Streaker rose from the seat and offered Allfores his hand.

Allfores rose too and hesitantly shook the hand, social distancing restrictions forgotten.

Once he was alone, he called Kate Allfores to warn her that Jonathon Bandip would visit her in the afternoon with details of a new posting. She was ecstatic. He imagined what could have happened had they been together and sighed.

CHAPTER SIX

Unexpected allies

The Prime Minister made a public statement regarding the relocation of the parliament outside Number 10. He stated that he would be discussing the project more comprehensively in the parliament and hoped that all members of the House would participate in the discussions. Afterwards, when he returned to his office, the phone would not stop ringing. The ministers wanted to speak directly to him about the relocation. Many complained that they should have been informed before the press interview. He fended off his party colleagues by telling them that it was a part of a clever strategy, ignoring the overwhelming fact that the Tories did not want to relocate. By the end of thirty or more calls, he felt exhausted but willing to take a last one.

His caller Helen Healthy was the only representative of the Green party in the parliament. Her dulcet tone unmistakable. 'I just saw your press interview, Prime Minister, and wanted to ask you why you're doing this.'

The question surprised him. 'I expected you to be delighted. Am I wrong?'

'No. I just don't understand why you've chosen to take the lead on an issue that is more usually acted on by your rivals, Rupert. I decided to ask you in the hope you might give me at least an inkling behind your reasoning?'

'I don't have an ulterior motive, Helen. We've been looking at this issue for quite a while. COVID has simply pushed it forward as a strong way to help the economy. Our relocation to

Blackburn will create thousands of new jobs. Besides, it will spur on the need to improve the nation's infrastructure between London and Blackburn. The project will probably be the biggest ever undertaken during this century. All parties will need to participate. The public will be watching. They're totally fed-up reading about us cocking up.'

'You mean your government cocking-up', she corrected. 'They're all down to you and your colleagues, Rupert.'

'Fine', he agreed. 'I want that to change. I want us to show unity while COVID is still out there. I want to give the public hope for the future.' He neglected to mention his hope of a large statue of himself erected outside the new parliament buildings.

Helen Healthy was shrewd and well-versed in the antics of other parliamentarians. She also did not believe that a leopard could ever change its spots. Streaker was a breed of parliamentarian with a rigid political agenda. Doing good for ordinary people was a low priority for him. Guessing he had a deeper motivation than he was willing to share, she gauged that the parliament was about to be hit by a load of government bullshit. A section might believe him, others would want to believe him, and then there would be the group of ministers who would refuse to accept anything he said. She would be included in the last category. Did it matter? 'I take it that you're going to speak to us all about your plans in the very near future?'

'Of course. Tomorrow. Will you be present?'

'Of course. I'll be as interested as everyone else to hear your proposals. Will they be focused just on the relocation of the parliament? Or is there something else?'

'It wouldn't be right for me to give any of the good bits away until everyone can be told at the same time, Helen.'

'You can't blame a girl for trying.' She chuckled.

'Are you likely to be supportive, Helen?'

'Depends what the good bits you're hiding are.'

'Nothing likely to challenge your policies. In fact, I'm hoping that you'll prove to be one of our most ardent supporters. If things go the way I imagine, you could play a prominent role with the media.'

'If I didn't know better, I'd say that you were offering me a job, Rupert. You know that I already have one. I'm with a rival party.' She sounded more interested than someone in her position should be.

'You don't need to change parties to deal with the media. Whether any of us like it or not, we all need to work together. That includes talking to the media in one voice. When I lay out our plans tomorrow, you'll appreciate just how involved this is. How about breakfast in the restaurant before I go face the music. Say about 10?'

'You've tickled my interest. See you tomorrow.' The line went dead, and Streaker cradled the receiver, guessing she would already be contacting her party colleagues to discuss their conversation.

***

Later that same evening, two limousines parked alongside one another in the underground carpark beneath Hyde Park. Streaker climbed out of the Jaguar and into the back of the Rolls Royce in which Bear Beddia sat patiently, waiting.

'I almost thought you'd failed, Bear. Unthinkable I know, but it's been a while since we last spoke', Streaker said, making himself comfortable on the opulent leather seating.

'They were pretty clever at hiding their identities', he replied. In his late eighties, Beddia's grey-green eyes remained as sharp as they had been at half his age. Any expected decline in mental agility was also a misconception. Bear Beddia received the best physical and mental medical support money could buy, but it was more than that which kept him young in mind and body. He called himself motivated. Others were less charitable. The newspaper baron had destroyed thousands over many years, while building an empire unequalled by any world-wide rival.

Ruthlessly and without shame, he had now reached a point where he could topple governments almost at will.

'They', Streaker repeated. 'You mean there's more than one in the Cabinet?'

'I mean that my people tracked them from your cabinet to the individual receiving their material and distributing it when and to whom he wanted.'

'So, who is this individual?' he asked eagerly.

'Not so fast, Rupert', the other man replied calmly. 'The cost for this information is going to be significant.'

'I never doubted it, but my need is great. I am sure you understand.'

'Let me pass this by you. Say I have a friend who is currently being investigated by the Serious Fraud Office and need you to stop their investigation

189

going further, although it is becoming abundantly clear that this individual is as guilty as hell. Are you willing to intervene to stop them?'

'It won't be easy; these things never are, but it's doable. What's your point?'

'Say my friend was the leader of another great country and his name is synonymous with operating outside the law. If what he did became public knowledge, things would be very difficult for him. In fact, he might even have to step down and face prison time. We can't have that happen. It would do none of us any good. You know why.'

'Are my people aware of who he is?'

'Yes.'

'I see.' Streaker sounded less enthusiastic but imagined the future chaos that could be created by this one individual. Not someone who believed in going quietly, he would reveal secrets about high-profile people around the globe, which would rock the foundations of every establishment in existence. 'Do any of us have a choice?'

'Not really'. Beddia remained unfazed. He had already had the time to absorb all the possibilities and taken the necessary precautions to shield himself.

'If the public ever discovered my interference in this investigation, I'd be finished.'

'While you have a leak in the cabinet, the possibilities of that happening are heightened.'

Of course, Beddia was right, but that didn't make what he needed to do any easier, either to achieve or to survive. There was bound to be resistance from the Serious Fraud Office and Home Office. Preventing leaks to the public from either would take a humungous effort.

'I will help as much as I can. None of my outlets will print a word, and if they receive a hint that the story has been leaked, I'll let you know that the storm is on its way. It'll give you time to prepare.'

'He's made so many enemies in such a short time.'

'We all make enemies, Rupert. None of us reached where we are today by being nice. Nice is for losers. I know that you want to keep your public happy, so they remember you fondly. You're hoping to go down in history as a good guy, but it really isn't realistic. The best any of us can hope for is that the little good we've done is also recorded in history, though it will never offset the bad.'

'Either way, I need those names. I accept it.'

They didn't shake hands as a movie would have one believe. Words, in reality, were sufficient. Their agreement was already cemented. Beddia revealed the names, 'William Slippery, Margaret Quisling.'

'Bloody hell. Environment and Works and Pensions', he snarled. 'Who else?'

'You're not going to like this. It's Granger Shallow. Your so-called friend from that public school of note.'

'We were having dinner with him this weekend.' He slumped back on the seat, as if he'd been punched in the stomach. 'How could he?'

'Rivalry. He was a previous prime minister, not someone who would want to be outshone by a friend in the same position. Whatever his reasons, he is very dangerous to you, as are those two traitors working for him.'

'What's the name of the investigation you want halted?'

'Dark Cloud. I think someone at the SFO has a romantic bent. The bit that I omitted relates to Russian involvement.'

'Bloody hell! It just gets worse. Are the Russians aware?'

'Of course. Don't be surprised if a few more deaths associated with Novichok turn up around Fleet Street. You know what they're like. They don't take prisoners or leave any loose ends.'

'You realise they could kick-off a war if things get too much for the public to accept? What does our friend say?'

'He believes in your abilities more than you do, Rupert. The British public can be muted by the right man. He insists that's you.'

'This really is an all-or-nothing exercise, Bear.'

'For us, all, my friend.'

***

Alone in his office, surrounded by darkness, Streaker sat behind the grand desk he had so coveted. The moonlight alone sprinkled light into the room. Granger Shallow, his friend, had betrayed him. All those times he acted supportive were only a ruse. Streaker felt numb. After an hour, a tap at the door brought him out of his gloom. Jonathon Bandip stepped inside and switched on the lights.

'Sorry Rupert, I didn't realise you were sitting in the dark in here. Are you alright?'

'Not one bit. Take a seat. We have a lot to discuss.'

He told Bandip everything and watched the other man absorb the information like a blotter. By the time he had finished, Bandip was already in the process of setting up a fresh round of plans. 'Well, first off, we need to dump Slippery and Quisling ASAP. I'll form a set of words for you and check who you should replace them with. Granger Shallow is different, I appreciate that. It's personal. Do you want me to deal with him, or do you wish to do it yourself?'

'I'll do it. Jessica and I are meeting him for dinner this weekend. I'll get her up to speed. He won't know what hit him.'

'It'll create a rift in the party.'

'It's already there, only hidden. This will just bring it out. Easier to deal with that way.'

'I'm sorry, Rupert. I know how hard it can be when someone like Granger turns out to be a rogue. I know how much you like him.'

'I know they say you can't fully trust anyone when you are in politics, but I thought Granger was different. He fooled me. Makes me wonder when he actually turned. Was it before I even became the prime minister?'

'What about the SFO investigation?'

'Tread carefully. Before we do anything, I need to know all they have and where they're at. We can't afford any slip-ups.'

'On a lighter note, Kate Allfores is very pleased with you about her new posting.'

He smiled weakly. 'Nice to know someone is happy with me.'

'Also, a representative from the EU phoned to ask about your intention to relocate the government. They see it as a positive step and have offered to help in any way they can.'

'The bloody EU! Why the hell are they sticking their noses into our internal affairs? What is it they've figured out that helps them?' He scowled at the unwelcome news. Every fibre in his body warned him not to trust anything the EU had to say. If they contacted him this early over the intention to relocate, someone in Brussels had figured out a scam that would likely cost the UK dearly.

'Wondered the same thing myself. I'm still working on it,' Bandip said.

'I'm exhausted, Jonathon. I think I'll have an early night.' He climbed to his feet and left his fixer alone.

Bandip would work through the night to provide him with a form of words appropriate for sacking two cabinet ministers while including the identities of two replacements. He was tireless, hence his dream for a place in the sun, provided a nuclear war could be avoided.

***

The following morning, while waiting for Helen Healthy in the parliament restaurant, a coffee cooling in front of him, he was joined by Vanessa Vamp, a back-bench member of the parliament he had come close to dallying with more than a year ago. He remained undecided whether bad luck had prevented their flirting from going further or perhaps fate. Whichever it was, Vamp was very much his image of physical perfection. Her deserved reputation as a maneater was not something that detracted from her allure. In fact, it probably added to it. Not a traditional beauty, she remained devastatingly attractive in an overwhelmingly sexual way that ensured that her presence had men standing to attention wherever she encountered them. Raven-haired and blue-eyed, with the hourglass shape other women would have killed for even at forty, she looked sensational. Regular exercise had ensured that her body remained taut – a succulent, ripe fruit.

'Nice to see you alone for a change, Rupert', she said, occupying the seat opposite. As she removed her face mask, her rich, succulent, red-painted lips captured Streaker's full attention. He liked watching her speak, watching the way her lips formed words in a sensual way. She must have practiced pouting as an additional skillset.

'I'm actually waiting for Helen Healthy, Vanessa', he warned, hoping that she would flutter away before the tongues began to wag. He guess then that it might already be too late. Her perfume reached his nostrils in a wave of aromatic poison that teased him with infinite demands for desirable responses. Yet, the last thing he needed at that moment was for another scandal to reach Jessica's ears.

'Well, she isn't here yet, Rupert. It gives us time to catch up on the past. Why haven't you called me. It's been so long!' Her knee brushed his under the table, making him sit upright.

'Vanessa, it's been an incredibly busy time, as you well know. Besides, lock-down is what it says it is. None of us can afford the risk this blasted virus poses.' He hoped to sound firm. Decisive. Her knee capturing his against the table leg suggested otherwise.

'We almost became lovers the last time we met. I saw a side of you that the public never sees.'

'Thank god for that!' he growled. 'Vanessa, we really can't do this now.' Her knee remained stubbornly jammed against his as a knowing smile played at the corners of her mouth. Her blue eyes flirted with him as her lips parted to reveal the whiteness of her perfect teeth. With a flick of her head, she shook back locks of raven hair, so they lay on her slender shoulders, away from her face.

'When can we do this?' she asked. The smell of intoxicating perfume swept over him. His senses were reeling. Anywhere else, he would have taken her there and then. It simply wasn't fair. She was enjoying his awkwardness too much, like a cat playing with a mouse.

'Perhaps never, Vanessa. I'm a married man with a very jealous wife...'

'You're a man who enjoys living dangerously', she interrupted him, ignoring his failing defences. She painted for him an image of lovemaking that she knew he desired. 'We're both the same in that way.' She leaned forward so that the ample cleavage hidden beneath a black jacket and blouse appeared, about to spill onto the table in front of him. He swallowed loudly, hoping not to dribble. 'You know you want me as much as I want you. I love power, and you're the most powerful man in the country.'

'I certainly don't feel like it at this moment in time', he said in a small voice.

'Rupert, I didn't know you'd invited Vanessa as well'. Helen Healthy stopped by their table, staring down at the pair.

'Sadly, Helen, I wasn't invited', Vamp snapped, annoyed by the intrusion. Just when she was doing so well! 'Call me, Rupert. You know my number.' With that, she rose and left them alone.

Healthy slipped into the seat warmed by the other woman. 'One of your conquests Rupert?'

'More like she was attempting to make me one of hers. For a long time, might I add.'

'It's so easy to make mistakes of that sort. That's what makes us human', she said. 'But she was being honest about liking powerful men. She has a string of lovers in the business world – all of them fat cats.'

'You appeared at the right moment', he said, watching Vamp's delectably rounded rear disappear out the exit.

'You can rest assured that I won't be spreading any gossip. This place has enough without me adding to it. So, any secrets you might have are safe with me.' She smiled.

'So, I hear', he said. It was true that several of his colleagues had mentioned Healthy as one of the most trustworthy friends anyone could hope to have. Making a friend of her promised more benefits than might ordinarily be expected. He had been playing with the notion of improving their relationship for that reason and also because he wanted someone on the other side of the House to discuss the relocation without any fear of compromise. A sounding board without an echo. She had been a member of the parliament for almost two decades and knew how to play the game better than most. For a Green party member to last so long was a credit to her skills as a politician.

'I'm sure the rumour mill began working overtime the moment she joined me. Jessica will already have heard.' he said glumly, imagining his wife waiting for his return.

'Well, if you need an alibi that nothing untoward occurred, tell Jessica to give me a call.'

'I appreciate that, Helen. Thank you.' They were joined by a waiter who took their order before Streaker spoke again. 'I'm sure you caught my drift from our last conversation.'

'You could clarify exactly what you were saying so that there are no mistakes.'

'Of course. I'd like the Greens to lead on environment issues surrounding our relocation. How we can keep the air clean while providing jobs to the local community, that kind of a thing.'

'Are you suggesting a partnership?'

'No. What I'm suggesting is that the Greens gain deserved public visibility for making worthwhile recommendations that we'll seriously consider. Meaning that we promise to take up any that we're capable of implementing. By directing your recommendations directly to me, you're assured that they will be read and considered. Call it a mutually beneficial unwritten agreement. I promise that any credit your party is due will be endorsed by this government.'

'That's very generous of you, but I'm a little confused as to why you would offer us such a thing. We're on opposite sides.'

'Not in everything', he said. 'We both have the interests of this nation as our priority. However, I'm well aware that this government alone cannot achieve all that's required by itself. We need to meet our political rivals halfway and, in doing so, make a better job of it than we might on our own. I see this as a massive project that is actually too big for one party. The numerous issues would, I feel, receive a biased priority from my side at times when we need a broader approach. That's achievable by communicating ideas without the fear of them being inconsiderately dumped into the bin. For that reason, I want your input-on environment issues and, through close liaison with my office, for all media reporting to be presented in a united way.'

He saw her drinking it all in. The possibilities of gaining public visibility for successfully achieving a safe environment while maintaining a high level of employment was a rare opportunity that she could not resist. It was a shame that he would ultimately be the one to fail her. His party would only go so far before they inevitably pulled the rug from under her. Any credibility the Greens might have gained would be lost when his party deemed that they had been used to the point where they offered no further advantage. It was how they operated. Toying with the notion of being considered a friend was simply a method he used to put himself in the right frame of mind. He had long ago discovered that achieving success at anything required a specific mindset. At the moment, it was befriending the leading politician of the Green party. It would be something else tomorrow.

'I'll have to discuss this with others', she said, breaking into his thoughts.

'Of course.'

Their food arrived, and they chatted about other subjects outside politics.

***

Afterwards, as he was being driven back to Number 10, his mobile beeped. Kate Allfores spoke quickly, 'I just heard that you were with Vanessa Vamp.'

'Good grief, Kate! You're risking everything by calling me just to express your awareness of the fact that Vamp sat down at my table this morning.'

'Vamp makes every woman concerned, and for good reason.'

'Well, you don't need to be. Vamp was simply trying it on, but I defended myself against her intoxicating assault with the bravery and cool of a true statesman.'

'That's not what I heard', she said. 'You looked quite flustered by her and was saved by Helen Healthy.'

'Not true. Well, not entirely. I'd arranged to meet Helen there, and she was late. Hence, Vamp took advantage of my being alone by thrusting herself into the seat opposite mine. I was completely innocent. A victim if you will.'

'That's not all she thrusted at you. A friend recorded the two of you. Those enormous boobs were given an airing too, weren't they?'

'Good heavens. I should've guessed that you had a secret camera in the parliament restaurant.'

'Just good spies.'

'Nothing happened. She left as soon as Helen arrived. Don't make a mountain out of a mole hill. By the way, where are you?'

'Still at the Kent nuclear fallout shelter. Jonathon told me to remain here until my appointment becomes public knowledge.' He marvelled at the fact that the rumour mill still managed to reach her even more than a hundred feet below ground. 'I'm not angry, Rupert. Just disappointed that I wasn't there to fend her off.'

'You know I always carry you in my thoughts, Kate', he replied in a super smooth tone that even end up impressing himself. Exaggeration had become so normal that it hardly registered with him. She was, after all, just another notch on his splendid weapon.

'Ah, that's so sweet. Did she reveal her stockings and suspenders?'

'What? Whose stockings and suspenders?' he asked, suddenly confused.

'Vanessa Vamp's silly. She always shows off a leg to her intended conquests.'

'Well, she must have realised I wasn't willing to be invaded. I didn't get a leg show', he replied. Pity. Imagining Vamp in black stockings was too wonderful a prospect for him to absorb without giving himself away. 'Anyway, how do you know she wears stockings and suspenders?'

'I have it on good authority', she replied. 'Promise me that you're not intending to meet with her for a shag.'

'I promise I haven't arranged to meet with her for a shag. Look, this is all quite ridiculous. I'm simply not interested. She said something about liking powerful men and that I was the most powerful in the country. It was all BS. You know how she is.'

'Everyone knows how she is!' Allfores snapped. 'The woman's a predator. Worse than anything the aliens could send! I just want you to be careful, Rupert. There's no knowing what you could catch from someone like that.'

'Honestly, Kate, I won't be going anywhere near Vanessa with my old man. Besides, Jessica would find out quickly and we know what will happen after that. Gosh, it's hard enough with the two of us cavorting when we get the chance. My nerves couldn't stand me doing it with anyone else.' He lied so easily even he believed it at times. If an opportunity with Vamp ever did present itself, he knew exactly how he'd react.

'Ah, you do make us sound special.'

'We are my darling. We are.' He wondered if he still had Vamp's contact number.

***

His return to the office was as he imagined it would be, with Jessica waiting for him there. Bernice Walters stood beside his desk, next to her. An expression of uncertainty was clouding her usual confidence. It struck him as odd that the one person who unnerved his personal secretary was not some dictator but his wife. Or maybe his wife was one?

'I told Jessica that your diary was full this morning, but she insisted on being here when you returned', Walters told him without moving.

'Thank you, Bernice.' He looked at his wife. 'Before you say a word, I know what this is about. Bloody Vanessa Vamp joining me at the restaurant this morning, isn't it?'

Walters gasped at the mention of Vamp's name. Even she felt threatened in some way, which was ridiculous.

'You're not surprised.' Jessica sat motionless, studying his body language.

'Why should I be? The rumour mill is notorious. I knew the moment Vamp joined me that her presence at my table would be irresistible to the gossip mongers. Hopefully, you received a comprehensively correct report of our encounter and know that I'm completely innocent.'

'I wouldn't have thought otherwise, my love. I'm just here to make a statement that my sources are alive and well and always looking out for my interests.' She climbed out of the seat, pecked him on the cheek, and disappeared out the door.

He turned to Walters. 'Panic over, Bernice.'

'Sorry Rupert, but whenever I hear that woman's name, a cold shiver runs down my spine. She'd have done well as a brothel keeper rather than as a minister of the Crown. It rumoured that she's been with so many rich and powerful men that she can call on any of them at a moment's notice to ask for a favour.'

'I must remember to include that on her CV the next time she applies for another posting.' He chuckled.

'To be honest Rupert, I sometimes don't know how you do it, managing to dodge these grabby women while running the country at the same time. It must be extremely hard. You must need nerves of steel.'

'I suppose I must.' He smiled. Walters doing his ego some good was unusual. 'I suppose I was born lucky.' He took his place behind the large desk and oddly felt at peace with himself. He was halfway to getting the Greens to support him, which, if successful, would be a first for a Tory prime minister. The encounter with Vanessa had revealed the extent to which he was under scrutiny. Even nuclear fall-out shelters were included in the rumour circulation list. A brief recollection of Vamp's delectable rear before she disappeared made him pout. A buxom woman – just the way he liked them.

Walters stepped out of the office to collect his latest African visitor, the Nigerian minister of industry. Adewale Kate stepped into the room with Walters behind him. As the two men made themselves comfortable by the open fireplace, she asked. 'Would you like tea, sir?'

'How could I visit the prime minister of your country and not accept a cup of tea?' He chuckled. Removing his mask, he asked, 'Not breaking any rules doing this, am I?'

'Can't stand the bloody things myself, so I take it off whenever no one's looking.' Streaker chortled. 'We can have something stronger to drink later.'

Walters left them alone to fetch refreshments.

'Good to see you again, Adewale. It's been far too long. I've been reading about this big music export of yours, and of course, if there's any way that my government can help, we'd be only glad to do so.'

'Actually, there is something', he admitted with a bright white smile.

Behind them the door opened, and seven-year-old Johnny Streaker ran into the room. 'Hello daddy.'

'Good heavens, Johnny! What on earth are you doing interrupting daddy when he's busy?'

Johnny ignored his father and stared at the other man. 'Who are you?'

'My name is Adewale Kate.'

'Kate's a girl's name. You're not a gender bender, are you?' The young boy looked far too young to appreciate what he was asking.

In a surprised but calm manner, Kate shot a look at Streaker before replying, 'I have children just like you. Always putting their foot where it shouldn't go. I've lost count the number of times I've ended up apologising for them.'

'I'm so sorry, Adewale. Please give me a moment to hand this young man back to his mother. Not another word, Johnny,' he said, snatching him by the hand and heading towards the open door before anything else popped out of his mouth.

'He's black, daddy', Johnny's keen observation continued, unfazed by his father's interception. 'Is he here looking for a handout? You said it's why they all come to our country.'

'Don't be silly, Johnny. That's not what I said. Next time, you listen properly.' *Damn*. He felt his skin turn red with embarrassment. His own son was derailing what should have proved to be an easy negotiation.

'I've got a photographic memory, daddy. It's exactly what you said. You also said they breed like rabbits and will overtake the white population. I remember everything you teach me, daddy.'

Streaker clamped a palm around the young boy's mouth as he frog marched him out of the room and handed him over to a security guard. When he returned, Adewale Kate was on his feet, ready to leave. 'I'm so sorry for that, Adewale.'

'No, it's fine', he said. 'Out of the mouths of babes. I'm afraid that I have to cut our meeting short, Rupert. I just remembered that I have something else to do.'

'But we haven't even started. You haven't even had a cup of tea.'

'No, but I wouldn't want you to think that I was only here for a handout, Rupert.' He moved towards the door as

Walters entered, carrying a tray with refreshments.

'Mr Kate, leaving so soon?' she asked.

'Yes. I've an appointment with the Chinese later today and need time to prepare.' With that, he shot out the door and was gone before either of them could delay him any further.

'What happened?' Walters asked.

'Johnny Streaker just caused a diplomatic incident, Bernice. You can take the tea away. I need a whiskey!'

***

The dinner party with Granger Shallow and his wife included four other friends. With Jessica fully aware of what had been happening, they arrived last, ten minutes late. It was his strategy. Not that they wouldn't have received the attention of everyone present anyway, but arriving unfamiliarly late suggested something important had caused a delay. All attention was on Rupert as they entered the large luxurious dining room with the other guests already seated around a large red wood table covered in a white cloth, with silver cutlery laid out. Each one was smiling. Friends, one and all. No face masks. Behind closed doors, they were free from scrutiny. The rules could be ignored.

'Our apologies for the late arrival', he said from behind a face mask.

'Let me take your coats', Betty Shallow offered.

'No need. We simply stopped by rather than telling Granger on the phone that I found out what he's been doing behind my back, how he's been attempting to undermine me with my own cabinet. It's all rather unsavoury really. Not the kind of stuff chums do to one another. Not real chums.'

Granger Shallow turned white. His wife frowned in confusion. She was possibly innocent in all this. Her hands caught in mid-air as she reached to help them with their coats.

'At least you aren't attempting to deny it. For that, I'm grateful,' Streaker said. 'This relationship has now ended. Your two accomplices are being sacked as we speak, and their replacements are being informed of their promotions.'

'Rupert, let me explain', Shallow said, quickly recovering from the shock. 'It's not what you think.' Shallow was a brilliant PR man – someone with the ability to recover from the unexpected without wasting time. Unfortunately, that's all he was. He had never possessed Streaker's imagination or innovation and instead relied on other

225

chums to steer him. He had been the face of the Tory party over several years and had stood aside when the situation appeared too tough even for his silver tongue.

'Please don't, Granger. There's no point. It's over. You're done, and by the time I'm finished, any hope you might have had of returning to politics should be forgotten. At least while I'm prime minister. There really is no place for you.'

'Rupert, Granger, I don't understand?' his wife said, turning to Jessica. 'What's going on, Jess?'

'Ask Granger,' Jessica said in a bitter tone that sharpened the sound of his name. 'I'm sure his story will prove entertaining. You're collateral damage. Same as me. We don't count when it comes to the ambitions of your husband.' She turned to the door, pausing momentarily. 'I had quite a speech to launch at you, but in the end, it's simply not worth it. Your husband is nothing other than a grubby two-faced piece of shit. Something I'd expect to find on the sole of my shoe. You can keep him.'

The other guests looked embarrassed and uncomfortable, wishing they were elsewhere. It was to be expected and seemed to fuel Streaker's performance. 'One last thing. Remember what you did at your inauguration to our university club? It was filmed too. I've heard that some photographs were found. There's every reason to believe that they'll be displayed on some nefarious website for the entire world to see. I wish you luck after that happens. You know how difficult it made things for me. You should explain what you did to Betty before the press does.'

With that, the Streakers turned on their heels and left, with Jessica Streaker calling out, 'Bastard!'

***

By Monday morning, Bandip had obtained a copy of the SFO investigation and passed it to Streaker. The case was further along than expected, with credible evidence pointing towards the one person in the world both he and Beddia had hoped to avoid. Whatever they did would be picked up by the system. The home office, the police, and even the security services had revealed interest in the case. Whatever they did would become known to all of them. Why they did it might be a subject of speculation, but there was little doubt the truth would be known. Keeping that truth hidden was going to be more than difficult. Beddia had not been joking when he had claimed that there would be a significant price to pay. He doubted that the newspaper baron joked much. His brand of businessman lacked ordinary humour. The kinds of things he found amusing usually included someone else's suffering.

Bandip returned to Streaker's office after allowing him time to read through the report. Taking the seat opposite to the prime minister, he said, 'Damning stuff. However, I think there might be a way of stopping it without us risking exposure.'

'I'm all ears, Jonathon.' He sounded as desperate as he felt.

'We feed in another lead, something that takes them to an alternative reality. One in which our friend is uninvolved.'

'You mean he'll appear like a scapegoat. As if someone else were trying to fit him up?'

'Why not?'

'You have the people who can do such a thing discretely?' It was a question he already knew the answer to but felt necessary to ask aloud, nonetheless.

'They're waiting for the nod. We have all we need to know from the report. They insert clues to head off the investigation and have them going round in circles until they realise it's a Russian scam.'

'You're using the Russians?' Streaker asked, the irony not wasted on him.

'They're only ones we can rely on.'

'Bloody hell. If our security services ever discover the truth, we're dead. This is treason. The Queen will be so disappointed.'

'No one will find out. The Russians are very good. They know to keep several steps ahead. I promise it's a good plan that will work.'

'But what will they want in return?

'Nothing that we can't afford.' Bandip was surprisingly knowledgeable about Russian demands.

'Please tell me you're not working for them, Jonathon', he asked, studying the other man very closely.

'I promise I'm not, but our paths do occasionally cross, and it is possible for us to sometimes help one another. This just so happens to be one of those times.' Bandip met Streaker's gaze, saw the doubts, and ignored them. 'Or we can tell Beddia that you can't help him.'

'Crap!' Streaker gasped. 'Between Beddia and the Russians, I don't know who's worse.'

'If you want this done, they need the nod within the next twelve hours.' His tone was neutral. Bandip knew better than to push Streaker. The prime minister had a threshold that would stop everything in its tracks even if it meant he would be injured as a consequence. They sat quietly for more than ten minutes as Streaker played out numerous scenarios in his head. Using the Russians was a desperate move, but he had made an agreement with Beddia. It had to be done. No one reneged on a deal with Beddia, not unless they were prepared to lose everything, they had spent their entire lives building. The stakes couldn't have been higher. *It is odd*, he thought, *how we have arrived at this point*. He had not seen it coming. Only Bandip had possessed a panoramic view of all the players. He could have warned him earlier about the Russians but had clearly avoided doing so because he wanted him caught in a net that he couldn't possibly escape. The question was why.

Streaker hesitated a moment longer before replying, 'Give them the nod.'

Bandip left. Streaker shook his head. It was unbelievable that he had had to use Russians on the British mainland to save a foreign politician. You couldn't make this stuff up. A portrait of Winston Churchill seemed to glower down at him. He couldn't meet its gaze and turned away to stare out the window.

A beep on his desk laptop signalled the arrival of an email. It was from Helen Healthy. It contained a suggestion that her party wanted considered with the relocation of the parliament: the use of sheep's wool to insulate the entire building. The wool was to be sourced from Northern Ireland, Scotland, and Wales. Their intention was to set a new precedent for the future of insulation for all new buildings. Doing so would silence complaints from Scotland that they would not receive much out of such a move other than for having a shorter distance to travel for their ministers.

Additionally, they wanted the new parliament buildings to be completely carbon neutral. To achieve that, they wanted the heating to be supplied through an innovative procedure in which holes drilled deep into the earth towards the core would be installed to receive and distribute heat. This would offer a natural way to heat the entire estate.

He leaned back in the seat. Innovation costs a fortune. Additionally, there were inevitably failures along the way to perfection, something his party would not accept. They needed to see investment make an almost immediate return. Long-term investments were abundant. It was the short-term ones that he was desperate to find. However, the idea of using wool as insulation could have something going for it. Having read a study on the health benefits of sheep wool insulation together with its low cost compared to some of the artificial insulations on offer, the proposal seemed to have merit. If he could persuade the cabinet to agree, Healthy would see him as meeting her halfway.

A second beep sounded as another email arrived. This time it was from an EU representative. They were interested in suggesting a joint venture for the construction of a rail tunnel between England and Holland, something that would dwarf the channel tunnel. Lowestoft to Zandvoort in the

Netherlands. The proposed tunnel would stretch about two hundred and fifty miles and require substantial investment. The building of this tunnel would significantly reduce the transportation chaos at Dover, the email reminded him. There was even a hint that the UK might be allowed to benefit from tariffs through the tunnel if it provided just ten percent of the total cost for the tunnel. *Are we interested in such a project?* Streaker chuckled to himself, tempted to agree, while wondering whether he would still be the prime minister in a week's time. It was something he needed to discuss with the cabinet and forwarded it to Bernice Walters to be added to the next meeting's agenda.

A reminder flashed up on his screen. He was due to meet the Nigerian representative Adewale Kate again that afternoon. The party hoped the relationship between them could be repaired to the state it was before his son's gaffe. The fact the Nigerians were being approached by China and Russia had the foreign and commonwealth office worried. The UK needed to be seen to be the first and only country Nigeria received assistance with in its multi-million-pound export.

The final email was from Kate Allfores. A thank you with kisses and photograph of a tattooed Lassie on a pink background that he recognised immediately. Pressing delete, it seemed probable to Streaker that they would share time together quite soon even though he hadn't planned it that way.

***

Two weeks later

'Immigration remains high even with COVID restrictions', the home secretary offered as the rest of the cabinet listened. No one appeared happy to attend cabinet meetings these days. Doom and gloom were ever-present in the atmosphere. Only the prime minister appeared content with the way things were. 'Brexit hasn't yet handed us a decisive method of cutting of the flow of immigrants, partly because of those being ferried across the channel by criminals but also because our borders remain too open to abuse. That's especially true with regard to the Republic and Northern Ireland.'

'Additionally, the Scots appear to be headed towards another independence referendum. The public have been listening to their government, and the latest figures suggest a fifty-five percent leaning towards independence,' Moon said.

'We may need to draw up contingency plans in the event they gain independence. Border controls will be a priority. I want it to be as difficult as it can possibly be for Scots to enter the UK if they win independence.'

'I have an idea', Dence said.

Streaker closed his eyes, wishing he were someplace else. 'What is it, Basil?'

'We rebuild Hadrian's wall.'

No one spoke. The atmosphere in the room was tense. Streaker stared at Dence, as if seeing him for the first time. 'What will we gain by doing so, Basil?'

'The Scots will find it difficult to enter the UK if there's a wall in front of them.'

'Walls don't always do well. The public has too many memories of the Berlin wall and of the one between the US and Mexico,' Hangready said.

'Basil has a point', Streaker unexpectedly said. Everyone turned to him, none daring to challenge him, none believing their ears.

'Additionally,' Dence continued with renewed confidence, 'we can use it as a tourist attraction by building it as it was. It kept the Scots out once; it could do it again, and we'd earn an income from it too this time around.'

'I think you might actually have something', Streaker told him.

Dence felt proud. It was probably the proudest moment of his entire life. The prime minister had praised him. It was a good feeling – one he had never experienced until now. Perhaps he could become prime minister himself one day and dole out praise when deserved.

'We need to make leaving the Union as tough as we possibly can. We must mirror what the EU did to us, giving no quarter no flexibility, and launch our own media campaign to undermine their leadership.' It was another big event during his time in power. Already the image of a second statue alongside the wall was emerging in his mind's eye. Perhaps history would refer to it as Hadrian and Rupert's wall. No, Rupert and Hadrian's wall. He couldn't keep off his face a small smile that showed his colleagues he was happy. 'We're making a statement to the others. Leave the Union at your peril. It's what the EU did so well, and we've got the scars to prove it.'

'It will also help the infrastructure north of Blackburn and generate even more jobs for another decade', Dence added.

'Wonderful', Streaker remarked. 'We're going to be loved by everyone except our rivals, who will be absolutely livid.' *This is indeed a day to be remembered*, he thought. 'Basil, I'll need some projections from you regarding costs and all the usual ideas regarding what's required in terms of manpower and equipment figures. This really is rebuilding this country.'

'There is just one point', Hangready said, interrupting the flow of happiness shared by Dence and Streaker. 'The Scots haven't voted yet. The polls might be wrong, and they could decide to remain.'

Like a whirlwind making a sharp turn, Streaker's expression changed. 'It might be worth to help them choose to leave.' His latest statue was already a memory. 'Very well. Basil go ahead with those projections. I want them ready in case I need them.'.

***

When Streaker next met with Bear Beddia, the newspaper baron appeared satisfied. he was as close as he ever got to looking happy. With the two of them sitting in the back of the Rolls Royce, he had a question that seemed to be foremost in his mind. 'Are you shagging Vanessa Vamp?'

Streaker frowned. 'No!'

'I heard she joined you at the parliament restaurant. Are you sure you're not shagging her?'

'I'm pretty certain that I'd have noticed, Bear. Not that I wouldn't. Chance would be a fine thing, but I've too much on my plate right now. Have you shagged her?'

'I've thought about it like most men, but she went with one of my close relatives and I have a thing about not shagging women who get too close to the family. They're dangerous. Finding out all about our little secrets. Next thing you know, you're up to your eyeballs in pay offs.'

'I take it that you don't recommend going anywhere near her then.' Streaker sounded disappointed.

'Quite the opposite. Fill your boots. She's absolutely gorgeous. Also, she could be of help to someone in your position. Knowing so much about so many is always useful, and given the right incentive, I'm pretty sure you could help yourself.' Beddia did not explain what he thought the right incentive might be, but he had sown a seed that made Streaker decide that it was almost time to act on the Vamp front in more ways than one. 'You've done well for me, Rupert. It will not be forgotten. Our mutual friend sends his best wishes and assures you that your future is bright, no matter how dark it may appear.'

Streaker, suddenly cautious, asked, 'Are you suggesting that things could get worse because of our interference in this investigation?'

'These things happen', Beddia said. 'What you must not do is panic. Remain calm at all times. Contingency plans have been put into place to counter whatever fallout transpires. You will always come out of it looking good. Be assured. The main point is to remain silent until I tell you otherwise.'

'This is all very mysterious, Bear. Can you tell me how bad it's likely to get?'

'What's the worst you can imagine?'

'Unthinkable', he replied.

'Of course, it won't get harsher than that.'

'Bloody hell!' he gasped. He wondered if he had been wrong in trusting Beddia and their mutual friend. Was he about to be dumped? It was impossible not to feel threatened, even though the other man did not appear fazed after explaining the dilemmas that lay just ahead. 'Are you telling me that someone knows what we did and that they're going to make it public?'

'It was always a risk', he said. 'You knew that when you accepted my offer. I promise you that you have nothing to fear provided you remain silent until the time is right. Timing is paramount, as it always is with these types of things.' The older man sighed. 'Trust us. I know that it is difficult sometimes, but we are better with you in power than anyone else. Hopefully, it's sufficient for you to understand that we are here to help you and not throw you in the fire.'

Streaker took in what he heard. Threatening retaliation if he went down was useless in this situation and likely to distance the only help available. 'Very well. Can you give me an indication of when things are going to begin getting difficult?'

'Tomorrow.'

'So soon!' He hadn't had the time to absorb what he'd just been told and now discovered that his entire life was about to be turned upside down tomorrow onwards.

'You can do this, Rupert. You've already proven yourself capable of much more.'

He just wished he didn't have to do it.

CHAPTER SEVEN

Unknown Depths

Tomorrow began as any ordinary Friday. Other than the fact that Streaker felt unfamiliarly nervous.

'Is everything alright, Prime Minister?' Walters asked as she stood in front of his desk, watching him bite his nails as he read a report about Hadrian's wall.

'Yes. Yes, of course, Bernice. Just glad it's Friday. It's been a long week.' He shifted as if in discomfort.

A knock at the door interrupted them. Bandip entered, followed by an unfamiliar tall reedy man, dressed in black. The man looked like an undertaker, and Streaker knew the worst had begun.

'Sir Reginald Rheostat from the ministry of internal affairs to see you, Rupert. I understand that you weren't expecting him, but he's here under direct orders from Her Majesty.'

'I've never heard of the ministry of internal affairs. Is it real?'

'Few people ever learn of us, Prime Minister. Unless they're in the worst kind of trouble. As you and your close staff all are. Please close the door, Bandip, and remain here with Walters. All of you need to listen to what I have to say.'

Bandip glanced at Streaker, who nodded before he closed the door. Rheostat remained standing. At six foot three, he stood head and shoulders above Walters, who appeared confused and nervous. By contrast, Bandip wore a blank expression that gave no hint about what he was thinking.

'I've been sent because this office – your office, Prime Minister – has been involved in treason against the Crown.' Streaker opened his mouth to speak, but Rheostat stopped him with a wave of his long-fingered hand. 'Please say nothing at this point. Just hear me out. It really is for your own good.' He had their undivided attention. 'Interference in an ongoing criminal investigation is where this begins and ends conspiring with a foreign country to hide the truth. The foreign country in question is Russia. Treason is when my office enters the fray.'

'You do realise that I'm the prime minister of this country?' Streaker asked, scrambling for the high ground.

'As I just mentioned, Prime Minister, the very reason I'm here is because this office is involved in treason.'

'What proof do you have?' he asked.

'Sufficient. Please do stop attempting to be above this type of thing. All I wish to know is whether all of you are involved?'

'Surely you don't think I'd be involved in such shenanigans?' Walters retorted.

'Personally, Walters, I would have said no, but until the culprits step forward, you are a suspect. You may even wind up as collateral damage. Which would indeed be a shame.'

'What does that actually mean?' Streaker asked with a frown.

'No decision has yet been taken regarding what is to be done with you.'

'What's the worst that could be done with us?'

Rheostat studied him for a long moment before offering a reply. 'A motoring accident is considered an easy way to disavow responsibility. Could happen to anyone unlucky enough to be in the wrong place at the wrong time.'

'You mean you'd murder us?' Walters asked, falling into the seat opposite Streaker.

'The public cannot discover that their prime minister or any of his close staff members were involved in treason. It is quite unacceptable. Could you imagine what it would do to public confidence in the government? Things are bad enough already without that headline being splashed across the internet.'

'I want to go home', Walters muttered, reeling from the possibility her murder was imminent.

'I'm sure that's what you'd like to do, Walters, but none of you are going anywhere until we resolve this matter one way or the other.' Rheostat spoke with such finality that none of them doubted the fact that he would keep to what he said.

For Streaker, it meant that his dreams of statues were in danger of remaining just that: dreams. How things would work out in the future appeared unpredictable. All he could hope was that Bear Beddia would prove true to his word.

THE END

About the Author

Born in the early fifties travelled extensively across the African continent going with his father who was employed by the British government. Settling back in the UK in the late fifties. He spent forty plus years in public service before retiring to Northern Ireland with his wife, four kids and collection of animals.

Enjoys fiction in these genres: crime, mystery, paranormal, science fiction, westerns, and witchcraft. Writes the genres he reads.

Other Books by the author

They're Having Another Laugh
(second book in the series)

The second alternative reality story relating to Prime Minister Rupert Streaker.

Prime Minister Streaker is determined to win public adoration to achieve a personal goal – a statue of himself erected outside the new intended relocation of the Parliament buildings at Blackburn Lancashire. Considering such a homage a fitting tribute for his premiership and something that will reflect in history suggesting that he was the best of the best.

However, to achieve his goal requires his political party to agree parliament's relocation, something most express great reluctance. Streaker finds himself at a fork in the road. He needs to continue to lead his party against fierce opposition if he wants to achieve his personal goal. However, problems mount as he includes the disbandment of the House of Lords that he intends to replace with a modern themed alternative that allows for commoners to become members. The kick back over such radical ideas brings out the worst in those most likely to lose out.

They're on the Move (third book in the series)

With construction for the new parliament buildings in Blackburn well underway resistance among British Prime Minister Rupert Streaker's own political party is reaching boiling point. Whether Streaker will survive until the new buildings are ready becomes a spectator sport as spin and hawkish actions try to unsettle him.

With his closest trusted colleagues Streaker finds himself at odds with almost everyone except those on the opposite benches who are uncertain whether to cheer him on at Prime Minister's questions or simply not argue.

Betty Buick - The Underground Mystery

Ninety feet below London a late-night tube driver goes missing while waiting at a red stop light. Abducted by aliens or ghosts seemed a reasonable possibility as far as the media was concerned. Of course, everyone in authority scoffed at such a notion. Everyone except DCI Betty Buick and her team at the Irregular Missing Person unit (IMP) New Scotland Yard.

Betty Buick – The Next Teen

Sometimes people go missing because they want out of a situation or are desperate to flee a harmful relationship. When it comes to teenagers you can add a romantic notion about being free and able to do whatever and go wherever you want. Then you have the missing who don't want to be lost. The ones targeted and abducted. They're the kids the police need to find before they're harmed. Trouble is the life-clock starts ticking the moment they're taken.

Fantastic Tales Book One

For lovers of Fantasy and Science Fiction. Three tales that challenge your imaginative limits. Lose yourself in the possible existence of Hell and what it might mean for those who find themselves trapped there for eternity in Soul Hunter. Alternatively, are humans unwittingly cohabiting with vampires, werewolves, and even triffids? Discover how monsters among us are trained to remain undetected in human society in Monster Boot Camp. Finally, did humans come from the stars to colonize the Earth? Were the creatures depicted in fables and legend real? Discover the answer in The Rings of Medusa.